I0684210

Pain & Panic

By

Joey Beauchamp

&

Jorge Harrington

Pain

&

Panic

JOEY BEAUCHAMP

&

JORGE HARRINGTON

COPYRIGHT © 2019 by Joey Beauchamp & Jorge Harrington

All Rights Reserved

ISBN: 978-0-578-62643-7

This book is a work of fiction. Names, characters, places and incidents are either the products of the author's imagination or used fictitiously. Any resemblance to actual events, locales, or persons, living or dead, is coincidental.

Introduction

For many years we have sat by the fire side telling stories that we conjured up from the darkest recesses of our minds. We sit on our couches enjoying the solitude of safety whilst watching horror films present us with some crazy killer's fantasies. We watch television shows such as *The Twilight Zone* and *Tales from The Crypt*, and if you were lucky to grow up in the 90's, *Are You Afraid Of The Dark*.

The horror story has kept us frightened and intrigued for many years. So why is it fear is a negative emotional aspect. If fear can grant such happiness in people, why is it thrown by the way side? As the great horror writer HP Love craft once said:

"It's a mistake to fancy that horror is associated inextricably with darkness, silenced and solitude"

We love horror deep in our hearts and love to be afraid of the unknown. What is lurking in the shadows, and what might decide your fate. That's what makes a good horror story, something that can successfully scare us, all the while prepping the reader to think. Reevaluate their emotions. Horror can bring people together in an unorthodox way.

We invite you to these eight truly scary stories from two different authors that are sure to stir emotions. So, tell your friends, and family, sit by the campfire, or turn off the lights and prepare to be scared. . .

Dedication

Dedicated to my wonderful Fiancé who never gave up on me, and of

course our son. I hope that one day you will be proud of me...

Table of Contents

A Sound Ever So Silent

By

Joey Beauchamp

The ship rocked back and forth with the sound of waves crashing against the old wood. Only the sounds of harsh waters could be heard in the night. Everyone aboard slept peacefully like a baby after a long day of crying. I had no idea the extent that this voyage would have on my life. All I knew was that I was fully invested, ready, and determined to make coin and go home to Virginia where I lived.

The voyage was nearly a year. That long of time on a ship, coupled with the lowest of men, made me even more homesick. I felt I did not fit in with this bunch of malefactors and rough individuals. Each person on the ship smelt like sweat and salt water. I tried my damnedest to keep clean while attempting to blend with the crew.

The captain was a stalky man, who stood over six feet tall, and had a long gray beard. His hair was natty, much like the Jamaicans in the Caribbean. His demeanor echoed someone of importance. He never disclosed his real name to the crew but instead only went by the title "Captain". His name must have been either fearful or embarrassing, because the entire crew were guessing it under their breath. He was the most mysterious man I had ever met. He must be linked with evil in some way. Perhaps he was saving us from what he really was. The crew worked without command. Did we respect him or fear him?

Whaling took a major effect on our ship. The beasts twice slammed their tails against the boat, cracking her starboard side. The patch we installed had held, but doubt infected the crew's mind. A whale's massive tale emerged from the dark ocean. It was the size of a large carriage or even a few horses. The tail glistened in the moonlight. The tail then crashed against the ship, making the sound of thunder.

It woke me from my slumber. I prepared myself for the sea to swallow me up. I grabbed hold of my blanket and braced. The water never came that night and neither did another whale. The ship yet again rocked me back to sleep.

As morning crept, I knew something strange was happening. The sun struggled to shine through the intense fog and dark clouds. Dark gray and mist filled the air. A depression fell over the ship and sea. We had not seen a whale for quite some time so any sound at sea was welcomed. We gathered our harpoons as the sound of blowholes could be heard. Despite being ready and willing to stick the first whale that got close enough, the crew was blinded by a gray veil. Everyone was quiet. The air was cold enough to freeze one's eyelids shut.

The voice of Captain could be heard loud and clear. We stood shaking in our boots, caressing our harpoons and tools. I had a hard time standing still as he spoke.

"Feel your way to the nearest mop, broom, and pail. There will be no whaling this day!"

I grabbed the nearest rope and began to ravel it along my arm. Ice pieces from the rope fell down to the ground. Just then, a sound of which I will never forget reverberated against the ship. It could be heard for miles. It didn't come from any whale, I was sure of it. If somebody could see my face, it was white as a ghost. With the sound, came a fast wind, that knocked us to our knees. Captain must be strong and sharp, because he didn't fall and still talked with his gut-wrenching voice.

"It goes below us!"

A roll call went out and everyone was present, except one. The sound was strong enough to rock the ship and send one of the crew members overboard. For ten minutes we called his name and there was no response to our efforts. The lad's name was Shamus. He could be a coward, perhaps fleeing in the dead of night in some sort of makeshift raft. The missing shipmate could still be in his bed or hiding in an empty wine barrel. Captain swore a great deal and ordered us to find him.

'He better be dead! Cowards get dragged by the neck below the keel!"

Shockingly, we never found him.

*****

As we sat eating our stale bread and watered-down chicken broth, the crew tried to frighten each other with their predictions. "What do you think it was?" asked one shipmate.

"I bet it was a Kraken," said another in response. "It's gonna rip us from the surface and drag us down into the sea."

"It could be a Megalodon. I've heard stories that say they can roar like that."

"Stop it!" I shouted.

"We hit a nerve lad? You getting girly on us?" asked the first shipmate. "We drag cowards by the neck."

"Not in the slightest," I protested. "Everyone lost their courage on deck, we should all be making our noose. I don't want to be scared if this is going to be my last night on this ship."

Silence went over the lunch party. There was no retaliation for what I said. They knew that whatever went below the ship, could drown us out of existence. No use dwelling on certain bouts of anger. This was surely a frightening situation. Not simply because of the creature, but fear of one's own future and mortality.

*****

Sleep didn't come easy for anyone. *What if the thing came back and turned the ship over? It would be like going to sleep and never waking up.* Nonetheless, we managed to grab some rest for a few hours.

The crew woke from the Captains loud yelling. "Get you arses up here! Right now! I never felt the stillness, come aboard and save me from my conjecturing!"

He's gone mad. I thought to myself. We raced up to the poop deck, some falling below from the rush. "Full Sail!" The Captain shouted. "Make Haste Lads!" Everyone raced to their stations. I grabbed the rope from the jib and released the sail. Soon we were speeding along the dark waters. We were headed into uncharted waters. *Where are we?*

"Captain!" I cried out to him. It had to be louder than the Captain's screams, so he would be able to hear me. "What are we running from?"

"Don't you see it! It comes for all of us!" His finger was pointing to the night sky.

My heart sank in my chest, because I did see what he was pointing at. A shadow in the night. It was blocking the stars and the moon. It was coming aboard, infecting each inch of the ship. The shadow was mist like, almost natural in color yet demonic. At first we assumed the shadow would pass until we witnessed a shipmate dissipate in the shadow. The crew tried to run back down into the cabin to hide. Some mates weren't so lucky to make it. Instead they were trampled to death. Stomped out of the world of the living.

I managed to make it below deck yet was pushed. I fell to the ground slamming my head on the side of a barrel. Blood fell from the side of my face. When I wiped the blood out of my eyes, I looked up and saw the shadowy mist picking up the crew members and ripping them away. Out of air as if they never existed. No trace of the men was left. They screamed in agony as they got absorbed by the shadow. As the shadow passed, I crept back up to the poop deck. "Watch out!" They yelled.

Captain stood at the helm, watching his crew disappear into the black death. I thought it would take him too. Instead he put a gun a to his temple and pulled the trigger. Blood sprayed out of the other side. There was no way someone or something would decide it was time to leave this world. He was the master of his own life.

There was blood and water everywhere. I went back below deck as the ship began to rumble. I grabbed onto what I could and screamed for my life. Just then a haunting sound came from the depths of the ocean directly beneath the hull. The ship began to crack on the sides. Soon I could see the dark sky in the crack. Wood, equipment, and water exploded into the air. My body was cast far into the air. I could feel the rush within my stomach as I plummeted back toward the water. I slammed into the black abyss knocking me unconscious.

*****

I awoke to a gull pecking at my head. Despite seeing the sun and feeling my back on the hot sand, I was confused and in pain. Sand was in the corner of my right eye and caked all in my hair. My legs were weak. It took me almost twenty minutes to get to a sitting position.

To my amazement, I sat on a tiny island. In the middle of it stood a dark cabin. The cabin seemed as though it had been there for quite some time. Perhaps built by the previous inhabitants some years back. I tried to cry out for someone from where I was sitting, but my lungs were sore and weak. It even hurt to breath.

When I did get to my feet and made it to the front entrance of the cabin, I knocked on the door as hard as I could. There was no answer. I tried the knob. To my amazement it was open. Inside was only a desk and a candle. The house was empty and dark oddly the sun did not shine through the wood. The entire cabin was only lit by the dancing flame. I came closer to the desk and saw an opened book. Its cover was green, and the pages were worn, looking faded and old in nature. It was a logbook, with all names of the crew. The ink used to write was dark black. To my shock I saw my name, Noah Golding Written next to my name was the word:

DECEASED

I screamed and the candle quickly went out. I thought about my biggest regret of the entire encounter with that sound. Was the thing that destroyed our ship a natural occurrence? Or was that thing always out there waiting for us? Did Captain know, or was he the one that made that mistake? What was Captain's real name? I grabbed the logbook and exited the cabin. As I opened the book again, I noticed the captain was not listed in the logbook...

He Rang

By

Jorge Harrington

Howie couldn't sleep. It had been twenty-four hours since his girlfriend, Morgan, packed up her things and left. *Is she really gone? Am I in denial?* After a while, he admitted to himself that he was spending more time playing video games, than spending time with his girlfriend. A three-year relationship down the drain, all because he couldn't stop playing. Howie had grown complacent.

His bed felt like laying on a raft in the middle of the ocean. No rescue boat in sight. The room was pitch black. Despite being almost thirty years old, Howie was afraid of the dark. Something he never told Morgan, but because of her, he found courage.

The house was five miles from the closest town. A big house with a large staircase and giant windows. It was too big for the Morgan and Howie initially. It now felt like a large prison cell. Morgan left while Howie was at work. It took fifteen minutes to realize that her stuff was missing. Still he knew instantly why Morgan left. It was because he wasn't paying any attention to her when he got home. He went straight from the door, to sitting and playing his game.

He thought that if he got rid of games entirely, it may fix some of the problems. Howie grabbed the console and ripped it out of the wall. He took the console outside and heaved it into the dumpster across the street.

Now that it was trashed, he believed the universe would tell Morgan that he "saw the errors of his ways" and would force her to come back. However, it did not work out that way. Now he lay in the dark in fear. A fear that he deserved. He neglected his girlfriend's needs.

Sleep almost came, but a light from outside shined through the bedroom window keeping Howie awake. Howie got up and looked through the window and saw the game console shining in the dumpster underneath the streetlamp. If the console could speak, it might ask to be lifted out of the garbage and be plugged back inside the house.

What if she never came back? She's being a little dramatic. She knows that I play a lot and said that she was okay with it.

He thought hard and starred at the game console protruding out of the trash. Should he go and get it? Maybe he was being a bit dramatic. Then suddenly, a vibrating sound could be heard. It was the sound of metal vibrating on wood. He jumped with a panic induced spasm at the sudden break in silence. He quickly calmed himself when he realized it was his phone ringing on the end table. A moment of excitement gripped him as the hoped it was Morgan. He picked up his phone eagerly.

An unknown phone number was displayed across the screen. A scoff of disappointment, Howie pressed the END CALL button and slammed the phone on the table in anger. *It could be Morgan's sister testing me,* he thought. She would support Morgan and would try and play mind games with him. A test to see if Howie would beg for her to come back. He already called and left a bunch of messages, eating up his phone's battery. It was after he filled her voicemail Howie began to feel like a creep.

The feeling of being creepy and unattractive, kept Howie in a constant state of anxiety. Watching television would be therapeutic and while he was watching it, he could come up with a solution. "Baby steps" he said. When he pressed the POWER button, there wasn't a reaction. He pressed in once more and the same result occurred. He then got up and checked the cord in the back. It was plugged in.

He then walked to his room and flipped the light switch. Again, no reaction. The room remained black, except for the light from the streetlamp. Maybe there was a power outage at his house.

"Damn it!" He yelled. He turned the flashlight on his phone and went downstairs to the power box. When he found the box, Howie noticed that his phone only had five percent left of battery life. There was no way he was going to be able to charge his phone, if he didn't get the house back up to par.

When he checked the power box, nothing seemed out of the ordinary. Howie tried all the switches and found that no matter how many times, or how long he switched them on and off, that the power box wasn't going to produce power. He would have to call an electrician, but there was no one available this late at night. It would have to wait until morning.

His phone vibrated in his hand, nearly making him drop it. It was the same unknown number.

"Hello?" answered Howie. His heart was pounding in his chest from anxiety. "Hello? Morgan, is this you?"

"I see you in the window," said a man's voice.

"I'm sorry, I think you have the wrong number."

"No wrong number," he said. "I see you at the window. I want you to let me in the house."

"Don't call this number ever again." Howie yelled. He was trying to sound tough, yet it came out as a whine. His thumb ended the call before the person could say another word.

As soon as he hung up, the phone began to ring again. "I said to stop calling me or I'm call the police!"

"Call em, they won't make it in time. I haven't seen a car in hours."

That sent shivers down Howie's spine, "What do you want?"

"Let me in the house. I used to live there."

"How stupid do you think I am?"

There was a sudden rustle on the roof. Howie ducked down to the floor. His lungs started to hurt, from holding his breath.

There was laughter on the other end of the phone. "I saw you get scared, it was so funny. Those were cats on your roof."

The voice on the other line must be close; to see on top of the roof. "Where are you?"

"Look past the streetlamp, I'm only a few yards from that."

He got to his feet and looked out the window. The amount of strain he put on his eyes to see past the lamp, made his eyes hurt. Howie saw a giant humanoid figure. Its arm rest on top of an old payphone box. He flicked his lighter and the flame from it; revealed his face. It was a horrific face.

"Don't I look pretty?"

*****

"I think you might be a little hard on him", said Charlie. She was sitting across from her sister. Morgan's phone was laying in the middle of the wooden coffee table, with missed calls from Howie. "He's called almost a hundred times."

Morgan didn't say a word. She just watched television like a drone, not listening to anything Charlie related.

"If you're not going to listen to your messages, can I listen to them?"

"Go ahead. I'm sure he can survive one night without me." She passed the phone to Charlie and sat back in the sofa.

*****

The giant at the payphone was hairy. His hair and beard were dark red, like a nest of red worms. His face was painted white and his nose was missing showing nothing but a hole where it had once been. The hole where it needed to be, was painted black.

Those features weren't what scared Howie the most. It was his teeth. Huge teeth that made the giant smile with bright cruelty.

"If you hang up this phone on me again. I'll marry you with this." The clown brought out a small double-bladed ax from behind him tauntingly.

*****

Charlie had finished a few of the messages that Howie left. Morgan looked like she was frozen in time. She didn't care that her sister was going through her private messages. Her eyes were glued to the television. The two sisters sat watching The Voice. There were a few love songs that almost made Morgan teary eyed, yet she stayed strong.

"Morgan, you have to call him," said Charlie, letting her emotions get the best of her. "He sounds like he's genuinely sorry for being an asshole."

"Let me guess," spoke Morgan, finally. "He sent me a long message saying he loves me, he's sorry, and he threw his games away."

"Pretty spot on sis, how did you know?"

"This isn't our first fight!" Morgan exploded like a shaken soda pop. "You have no idea how many times I've come home from work, just to find him sitting on his ass playing video games. He never asks me about my day or anything like that. Howie cares only about Howie."

I know that must be rotten," said Charlie sarcastically "You know men are like that. Have you ever tried to play some of the games with him?"

Morgan looked away and slowly shook her head. "I guess I never thought of it that way before."

"Sometimes we make dramatic decisions when we're mad." Charlie shrugged her shoulders.

After Morgan rolled her eyes, she gave thought to Charlies statement and finally caved in. "I guess I'll give him a call."

"Look dude, my phone is about to die," said Howie, frozen in place at the window. The clown was doing an amazing job of keeping him on the phone. "I gotta go"

"I will have no choice but to take back my house by force," said the figure. "I didn't think it through when I cut the electricity."

Howies worrying and anxiety was interrupted by his own thoughts. If he didn't calm down, he would most certainly have a panic attack. Is this really happening? What are you going to do Howie? You can call the police with the little battery you have left and get help. Maybe there is police car in the neighborhood. What about the neighborhood watch?

What if he gets inside the house before you can tell the police your address? Are you willing to take that risk? Make a choice already!"

He ended the call. It was already taking too long for Howie to dial 911. he pressed the number nine and that was when he heard the clown-like figure dropped the phone. It swayed back and forth and hung there dead.

*****

"It went straight to voice mail," said Morgan. She looked at her phone puzzled. "Maybe *he's* mad at me."

"I doubt that he's mad at you. He was leaving messages for you all day," said Charlie.

"We interrupt this program to give warning of an escaped patient from the Oregon State Asylum. An escape that has left officials scratching their heads. With around the clock supervision, patient Ian Zane was able to walk out of the building without detection. Your local police department will give safety tips on how to stay safe. "Here is a photo of the patient known as Ian Zane. Police say he might have altered his appearance. If you see him, let the authorities know right away. Do not approach, do not provoke, and above all else, do not speak to this man.

"He looks like an absolute nutcase." the picture showed Ian smiling. His eyes looked like they could cut ribbons and his long pointy nose poked out like a spike. It was the patient's teeth that haunted Morgan. They were giant teeth and they looked like they didn't fit in his head. His teeth gave him an evil grin.

The photo did nothing but creep the pants off the two girls.

"He's out there and Howie is all alone," said Morgan. Her hands went over her mouth.

Howie is going to be fine," said Charlie. "I don't think he's dumb enough to forget to lock his doors."

Morgan didn't listen to what her sister was saying. "I just wish he'd answer his phone."

*****

Howie's first intention was to run to the garage and drive away, except that wouldn't work because of the power being cut. There would be no way to open the garage door. He was trying to be smart about the whole situation, but he was doubting his ability to survive. The clown could be seen through the glass sliding doors and when it came into the light, the ax looked cartoonish because of how shiny and sharp it was.

How was he going to fight him off? He had no weapon and it was still pitch black in the house. Howie was shaky yet tried to remain still. He watched the clown come closer and closer to the glass door with the ax. The size of the clown blocked the streetlamp. The sound of the door moving was enough to get Howie's running upstairs.

A crash came from downstairs. It was the sound of glass breaking and wood splitting. Crunching sounds of the clown's feet walking over the glass and breaking it. Then it was quiet for a few seconds Then suddenly there was the sound of a bic lighter being flicked.

The lighter had lit a ball of light for the clown to search five inches in front of him. It moved around like a phantom light. To be spotted, would mean the end for Howie. Howie moved quietly to his closet.

The closet had everything in it, except a weapon. Howie was lucky the clown was carrying an ax and not a gun. *Or does he have one concealed?* Howie thought to himself.

He was going to have to go out the window and be out and on top of the roof. Howie grabbed the bottom of the window and jerked it upwards. The abrupt motion caused his fingers to slam against the wall, injuring Howie. While Howie was shaking the pain away, the ball of light was almost at the top of the stairs and so were the heavy footsteps. "Here he comes! You better hurry! Unlock the window and get the heck out of here. Have you ever felt an ax in the back?" Thought Howie.

Howie looked out the window and down to the street below. He then let out a loud shriek. The blade from the clown had struck Howie's back. He had already been halfway out of the window. Howie pushed his body out of the window but not enough to break free. He was escaping with his life. One knee was up, and he was about to do a push up that would get him to his feet, but he felt the cold steel in his calf. The clown struck Howie in the leg causing an instant pool of blood to form.

If he didn't get his foot out with the rest of his body, the clown would have successfully cut it off. Howie fell onto the roof. There was blood everywhere, yet Howie was surprised that he could walk towards the satellite dish on the roof. The pain in his leg caused him to limp slowly toward the satellite.

Will the clown be able to fit through the window? Was he safe with only the one injury?

As he limped toward the satellite, he saw the clown swing his axe at the window and create a hole. The clown stepped out and walked toward Howie. Howie didn't know if the clown was laughing, or if the alien sound was coming from the hole in the clown's face. Perhaps it was a bit of both.

"Get out of my house!" yelled the clown though his titanic teeth.

The satellites cord was loose, and Howie ripped it from the metal bracings on the side of the house. The dish was mounted with four bolts, making it strong enough for him to swing down to safety. There was still a fighting chance he would get out of this alive!

He could hear the heavy footsteps from the clown. Howie wrapped the cord around his hands and threw himself off the roof. He fell from the roof, but not before the ax struck his shoulder. It about tore him in half! His vision blurred from the pain. The added momentum caused him to spin, and the cord wrapped around his neck, catching him right before he hit the ground.

The clown looked at Howie in shock and amazement. The clown drove the axe into the side of roof, leaning on the handle, Ian Zane, the clown, pulled out his cigarettes and placed one between his gnarly teeth. It was on the third try that the giant clown was able to light his cig. He couldn't help but laugh at what happened. "Ironic" he said. Smoke came billowing out of the fresh hole in the center of his face.

*****

The next morning, Morgan and Charlie drove their dad's truck to Howie's house. They took their dad's truck, so they could use that as an excuse to leave if Howie attempted to keep them. They would say that they "needed to go because their dad needed his truck", if the conversation between went sour.

"What are you going to say to him?" asked Charlie.

Morgan shrugged her shoulders and did not give an answer to her sister's question. Instead she glanced over at the old phone booth that was near to their house. Seeing it gave her a bad feeling and she just wanted somebody to get rid of it already. Some weirdo must have used it because the receiver was hanging by the cord.

When the sisters arrived at the house only a moment later, they got out of the truck and froze. Howie was hanging from the roof by his neck, much like the payphone receiver. Morgan began sobbing, "HOWIE!"

The Letter

By

Joey Beauchamp

This letter was passed down to me by Doctor Gregory Tepeke. He told me it was a fabricated story given to him by a man that had "become mad". His name is George Gosovich. A retired veteran who states that something walks among us. Something that isn't humankind. Something unexplained. I thought it would be of great importance for you to read and learn what he saw that day. This letter is disturbing and makes me feel uncomfortable.

Sincerely,
Winston Elber

Date: 23, July 1919

Cambridge University Psychology Department,

Let me introduce myself. I am a student at this wonderful institution. My classes and schoolwork have all but been eye opening. My name is George Gosovich and I was born in the small town of Treasure Wyoming in 1899. As a young boy I enjoyed horse riding and raising the many farm animals on our small farm. We lived almost 80 miles from any establishment, so becoming anything other than a certified farmer was not in the cards.

I became obsessed with psychology, especially after my brother, who suffers from night terrors, had screaming tantrums almost every night.
Sweat would often be dripping from atop his forehead and the sheer terror in his eyes told me everything I needed to know. I knew in his heart that whatever dream that had accompanied his frightened demeanor, was true and genuine. I took it upon myself to conduct small experiments with my little brother every night and keep a journal of my discoveries.

The first night I took a feather from the barn and brushed it over his forehead. The tender feeling of the feather surely would have provoked a reaction. However, this was not the case. The gentle rub from the feather was simply too light. The next night I decided to use something harsher and sharper. I took a sickle from the barn and gave my little brother a poke. Not enough to break skin, but just enough to gain a reaction. Please keep in mind this was all for the sake of science. To my surprise, he did not wake. I concluded that my little brother was stuck in a trance that he couldn't escape. Some sort of sleep coma. I eventually grew bored of the experiments and went back to my bed. When I woke the next morning, pain shot through my back. I felt with my hands and could feel the scratches all over. They felt like they were overlapping each-other. A new pain and an old pain, simultaneously. It was strange, because the pain came the moment, I opened my eyes.

Where did it come from?

Perhaps they came from the hard work labor from the roof construction. The shingles were sharp and since I have a short attention span, I could have fallen and injured myself. I don't know where they came from, but I do know that this was the beginning of more questionable nights. I wrote the pain off as work related.

As days progressed, I often could hear chatter late in the night.

The voice sounded like a man and a woman but would scramble into one amplified voice. Then the voice would scream and then go silent.

Something different happened every night. Doors would open and shut. Windows would squeak open and close. Stray dogs would gather close by and bark uncontrollably. I wondered if I was the only one aware of it?

One night, my brother didn't wake from his night terrors and that scared me above all. How come he wasn't screaming? Did my work finally pay off? Is my imagination playing tricks on me?

Years passed yet strange things happened to me every night while my brother slept. I didn't know how much more of this I could take. I abandoned my family and joined the army. It was time to forget about all the night terror shenanigans and odd occurrences. I was only wasting my time, worrying about my brother, and needed to focus on my training.

In the spring of 1918, my training was complete, and my company was sent to war in Paris. The ever-escalating Battle of Aisne is one I'll never forget. When we arrived, our men were immediately flanked by German forces. The sound of bullets and bombs falling were all around us. One could not explain the horror I saw. Bloodied bodies lay next to the broken tanks. Some bodies so mangled that one could not recognize. Bashed faces, bloodied heads, and body parts. The sight caused me to become disengaged from the world.

When we entered the trenches for the first time, the walls were tall and full of worms, maggots and all other vermin. Some men were so hungry, they would gather trench worms and cook them in a pan. Piss, shit, and vomit covered the ground. The smell is something I won't soon forget. The smell gives me sleepless nights to this day.

As night crept and the cry and screams of soldiers began to dwindle, an eerie feeling came over me. I felt as though something was following me. The bodies that lay around me as I walked the trenches, seemed small. Are they dead or are they sleeping? I asked myself. I immediately thought of my brother. Did these soldiers with their eyes closed have night terrors too? Anyone could have had night terrors since this place was in fact, a place of sheer terror.

I then felt a presence behind me. A feeling as though someone was following me. I could feel it all over my body and in my bones. Behind me was something. Its massive shoulders blocked the path back to the other Safe Zone. The shadow this thing was producing from the moonlight, covered me with darkness. It was heavy and it was suffocating. My rifle shook in my hands. I felt as though was dying from fear.

Whatever the figure was, it did not see me. I thought it was a bear or some other beast from the town. By some miracle, I was able to gather myself and think of a plan to not be seen by this thing. If I was to stand still and not make a sound, it would pass me by. My weapon shaking and at the ready.

What is this thing? I remember thinking to myself. It looked like a humanoid grizzly bear. It was disgusting. The eyes were small and beady. They glowed like two rubies and matched the blood coming from its jaws. Traces of flesh and uniform were left on its claws.

I watched it come towards me, but still it didn't see me. How come I couldn't bring myself to open fire? Perhaps Lady Luck came knocking? If I just stay still and not utter a breath, I might stay alive.

Whatever I was doing was working. My stomach burned like fire and my forehead was turning red from how hard my heart was beating. The entire encounter lasted about one minute. It didn't see me at all. I don't know how long I was standing there until I was able to move.

I turned around and saw the monster disappear into the deep trenches. My fists were white from how tightly I was holding my gun. I'm glad that I didn't open fire, but I kept hearing screaming in the night. Was it that thing eating the men? Or was it the other side killing us with their bullets?

While walking back to the Safe Zone. I walked because I didn't want that thing to hear me. What if it heard me escaping and decided to come back and finish me off? Asking myself all these questions, I got lost and came upon a group of soldiers that raised their weapons at me in fear. The scary thing was the group of soldiers were the German Army. A group surrendering to one person?

I threw up my hands and thought of all the time I wasted, thinking I have come out of this situation unscathed. I closed my eyes and waited for the explosions, but instead only heard screaming. I could hear ripping sounds and gunfire. All the soldiers were dying at the hands of that thing.

My body fell from underneath me and I passed out. Lady Luck showed her face again, because I'm alive enough to write this letter. That thing is still out there? Every time I close my eyes, I can hear those screams and see that monster's face.

I am a student psychiatrist here at the University and am still unsure of what I saw. My brother died a few days after the war had ended. The scary thing is a new war is brewing, and I now suffer from night terrors.

Yours truly,

George Gosovich

Dragon Fever

By

Jorge Harrington

Savannah hit the snooze button on the alarm clock for the fifth time. Five extra minutes felt like winning the lottery. However, she didn't want to get up. If she got up, she would have to go and take care of her father sick bed-ridden father. There has never been a day that Savannah woke up and found dry sheets.

At first, taking care of her sickly father – whom is sixty-four – felt honorable. After the first week it began to feel like a chore. By the second month, Savannah was exhausted from all the sleepless nights and constant washing of urine stained sheets. She didn't know what was worse, cleaning up after an accident in his pants or cooking the same meals repeatedly. Her life was starting to turn into a scene from the movie Ground Hog Day.

There was no time for herself. She was a slave to her father's needs. How could she be so stupid as to even consider taking care of him? So she could get into Heaven? When was the last time she went out with her girlfriends?

The alarm clock went off again and this time, Savannah rolled her body out of the jaws of her comfortable bed. She did it fast for fear she would fall back into her war sheets.

*****

Her father, Ted, sat at the kitchen table like he was frozen in time. His sickness was a rare one – only three cases of it in the past six years. It started off as fatigue but eventually led to far worse complications.

Occasionally, Ted would stare off into outer space and forget where he was. His hand would become shaky and he eventually went blind. His eyes began to turn a harsh crimson red.

After a year, his eyes looked like two bright rubies. Savannah's mother had run off with another man as soon as she found out that Ted's health was declining. It broke his heart into a million pieces.

Savannah remembered the day she came home and found her mother leaving in a car. The man had a beard and had his arm wrapped around her shoulders. They both laughed as the car drove away from the house.

Sometimes, Savannah didn't know how she was still living, with the sort of pain she felt. There was barely any money and she watched as her father died slowly and painfully. There were no words to describe how Ted felt. His tears would turn red from the amount of crying.

Often, she thought about his sadness and it helped her to keep going. Humans are built for struggle and Savannah was tough.

"I made waffles instead of pancakes," said Savannah. "I thought it would be a nice change from the same old pancakes." She put a plate in front of Ted and placed his fork in his hand. "You need to try and fork the food yourself. The doctor said it'll make you stronger."

His eyes looked awful, thought Savannah. She took a seat next to him and began to eat her breakfast. Savannah tried not to look at her father's death stare while she ate her scrambled eggs and waffles. A glob of syrup drizzled down her mouth and it reminded her of the goop that was coming out of his eyes.

In a raspy voice, Ted began to speak. Unexpectedly, Savannah screamed, and she spat out her food back onto her plate. He had not spoke in a very long time.

"I inherited a land, "he said "When I die it will be yours. It was my grandfather's land. But I warn you my daughter of the events that happened there and pray you never go there. Will you hear me?"

*****

Savannah let her father speak. She was awestruck by his words, because he hadn't spoken in such a long time.

"There's gold in that land. It was found by two kids making sand castles, playing, and running. One of them tripped and fell over something protruding out of the ground."

"It was the size of a soccer ball after they had dug it out completely. One of them took their bucket to the lake to get water. They did this so they could soften the dirt and help them pull it out of the hole faster. The child that tripped over it, had hurt himself badly. But he was distracted by the gold they pulled from the earth."

"Their father told them bedtime stories of pirates and gold. They thought it all was make believe but clearly it was real. The kids had no time to investigate the gold further, their mothers had arrived and asked them what they found."

"The two mothers starred in wonder at the gold. They could sell this and they would instantly be out of poverty. What a blessing this was, and it was her child that found it. She thought since the child was wounded, she was entitled to the gold. Before she could make a move or utter a word, the other mother's hands reached to the golden ball and ripped it from the child's grasp. It was the gold that was making them act this way. The mothers were taken over by Dragon Fever. Greed so strong, that it brainwashed and ultimately destroyed it."

Her child that tripped over the gold, began to cry and crawl towards the mother. She kicked at all three of them. One of her kicks connected with the side of the child's right temple and killed him near instantaneously.

The mother's strangled each-other to death and the ball was dropped on the living child. It was horrible. For three days their bodies and blood stained the ground, until my grandfather sent out a search party to find them. The whole town looked for those families and it was the fathers that lead the search parties. Together they found the bodies. The fathers weren't ready for what they saw, their hands turned into fists and they cried. All the hype, and all the rumors, and all the worry, are true.

"It didn't take long for them to see the ball of gold laying on top of one of the kid's body. Somebody grabbed it and began to run away with it. He was stopped and was pushed backwards, and the new owner began to run."

"A fist stopped him, and he dropped the ball on top of somebody's toe. A domino effect began within the search parties and every ten minutes, somebody died. They were beaten to death or they were stomped on.

"By some miracle, one of the search party members lifted his fist and before he delivered it to his neighbor, he looked over to his left, beyond the fighting, and saw a figure that wielded a weapon."

*****

"I warn you not to go there ever!" he shouted. His eyes began seeping blood and puss.

Savannah lost her appetite and began to cry. The story her father had just told her took a hold of Savannah. She didn't know why. Perhaps it was because she thought her dad was left with nothing. He had something to give and he was giving it to her. She looked at her sickly father. "I love you dad."

*****

Ted died two weeks after he told the story. "Was it true?" Savannah thought. "Did he really own a land with buried gold?" She couldn't believe it. For those two weeks she thought only of the gold and the warning her father left her.

When they buried Ted, Savannah's mom didn't show up for the funeral. She didn't have to love her dad, but she could've come to show her respects.

A lawyer approached Savannah and explained that her father did indeed have a will. There was a list of things he left for her, but it was the Bill-of-Sale for a piece of land that caught Savannah's eye. Her father *was* telling her the truth after all.

It wasn't until Savannah was having money troubles, that she was entertaining the idea of going down to that piece of land and investigating. If she didn't pay the bill in a week, she was going to lose her father's house. It would break her heart if that happened. So, she went and grabbed a shovel and bucket and tossed them into her car.

*****

NO TRESSPASSING

The sign was metal and hot to the touch. Savannah placed her hand on the handle to the gate and quickly pulled it away. It felt like she was burned with fire. Awestricken she looked at the gate. "Hot?" she said. She went back to her car. She had to rummage through her trunk. She grabbed an old shirt so she could use it as an makeshift oven mitt.

She rested her shovel on her shoulder and let her bucket dangle from her left hand. When she pushed the placed her hand on the metal this time, she could feel a warm sensation in her hand with the makeshift oven mitt she made.

A screech sound echoed around her. It scared her and even the crows that were nearby. They squawked and you could hear them scurry away from the fear in the air. There was a breeze that blew past Savannah. It was hot and full of dirt so she had to close her eyes to avoid the dust.

If there were any signs that she shouldn't be doing this, she didn't do a good job of reading them. She opened her eyes and walked through the gate. It felt like a desert. It baffled her to see any sort of life growing out of the ground. There were tumble weeds and dead trees, but mostly hot sand. That wasn't what caught her eye, It was the lake.

*****

Her father's story bounced around in Savannah's mind. He was sick and didn't know what he was saying. He words became slurred. So far, he was telling the truth. Was that why she was scared?

What would she have to be afraid of? Scared of success? Or was it the deaths that kept her from being calm? All she had to do was go to the lake and scoop up some water. The water would be used to make the sand easier to dig up.

She pushed the shovel into the sand, so she could carry the water with ease. When Savannah looked at the water, she could see straight to the bottom. It was so clean and so clear. It made her smile. She made a cup with her hand and brought it up to her mouth to drink. It took everything for her to stop drinking and bring the water over to her shovel.

When she made it back to her shovel, Savannah poured the bucket out on the ground and watched as it evaporated into the sand. The Earth was so dry, that it took more than four buckets of water to get her shovel a few inches below the surface.

Beads of sweat fell into her eyes and burned them. She took the shirt and tied it around her head like a bandanna. She was determined to find something. Determined to find anything. Determined to find her gold.

*****

A few hours went by and Savannah was beginning to make progress with the hole she was digging. She was deep enough that the sand didn't swallow up the water right away. She didn't have to make multiple trips to the lake. She wished she had dug closer to the water, but according to the story, it was farther out.

The sun was doing a good job at making everything hot and miserable. Savannah took off her shirt to help her with the heat. She still had a tank top on, and it was soaked from her sweat. Her shoulders were starting to burn, from the work and she began to get a raging headache. If she continued to drink the water, she would have to go to the bathroom and there wasn't a place where she could go. The car was to far away. If she went back to the car, she was going to leave and possibly not come back.

But then Ted would lose the house and that's what kept Savannah going. She kept digging and digging, until she thought she would die of heat stroke and exhaustion. She felt like giving up, until she felt her shovel hit something hard and shiny.

There were no words for what she felt when she saw the sun hit the sliver of gold. She poured the rest of the bucket into the hole and the water uncovered the top of a golden ball. Savannah couldn't believe her eyes. It was going to be worth millions of dollars.

Savannah dug around it and a few times. She was hot and tired, but when the golden ball came loose, she felt a surge of energy and was able to lift it over her head and push it out onto the surface. The ball was heavy and she could barely lift it.

Her jolt of energy and sudden strength was a result of the Dragon Fever he father had told her about. She thought only of the gold. It was finally hers. All of it was hers. The land from which the gold came from was her own. There had to be more and that was hers as well.

She picked up the golden ball and held it to her chest cradling it like a baby. The soccer ball sized gold ball shined in the sun. It was beautiful. Savannah couldn't tell if it was her sweat or her tears that were dripping on the surface of the ball. She began to walk back towards the car and didn't notice that she was taking a different route.

The dirt she was shoveling out of the hole, had made a small hill to the right and was in the way of her old path. She walked a few feet off to the left and was preoccupied with her thoughts of how wealthy she was going to be. It must be more of the Dragon Fever. SNAP!

*****

Savannah didn't scream right away, because of the quickness of the bite. A bear trap had released on Savannahs leg. She fell to the ground with the gold ball. The ball landed on top of her chest and knocking all the air out of her lungs. Never in her whole life, had she felt such pain. Her leg felt like a broken branch, hanging on with splinters.

She tried to reach for her stomach and her leg at the same time. Her mouth was gasping for air and she looked as though she was a mime. It took a long time for her catch her breath and make moaning sounds from the pain she was in. When she looked at her legs, she could see that her leg was trapped inside the teeth of the bear trap.

How come there's a bear trap out here? That was the million-dollar question.

There was no doubt that there was metal on bone. It didn't break the bone, but it sliced right through her calf. She slowly got to a sitting position and examined the damage. It looked like her limb was in a car wreck. When her fingers touched the metal, she instantly regretted it.

Those horror movies where they try to pry open the teeth came to mind, as she attempted to pry off the trap and free her leg. Obviously, movies are fake, but Savannah had no other choice. She was essentially inside of a horror movie.

What was she going to do? Savannah cursed herself for being so stupid and naive. Stepping into a bear trap out in the middle of nowhere was an accident. She remembered she had made a mistake coming out here without telling anyone.

It wasn't long before she realized she wasn't alone. The sun began to disappear. It was starting to get cold. The cold was welcomed at first, then it began to make her teeth chatter. Savannah's jaw was beginning to feel like a rusty hinge. The dry blood looked like paint that was chipping away from wear and tear.

That's when Savannah looked at the lake and saw a black hood pop out of the ice.

*****

Her father's voice could be heard inside her head, *"a shadow that hovered and wielding a weapon."*

The shadow was Death and the weapon it wielded is a scythe. It was faceless and had no flesh on its hands. Death floated towards Savannah without a sound.

Savannah knew if she didn't get out of the trap, she was going to die. Losing her leg was better than losing her life. She was going to have to shut the trap completely and surrender her leg This would ensure her escape.

She took the mark shift bandanna from her head and wrapped it around her leg. It was hard to pull the knot tight with how cold her fingers were. Death's hand reached out at her but before it could grab her hair, she slammed her fists down on the trap and snapped her leg off.

It felt so good to be free from the trap. Savannah was more relieved than she was scared. She could feel the cold on her back as she crawled towards the car. Blood trailed behind her. Death gained on her closer and closer.

Her freedom was cut short, when she saw the golden ball blocking her path. Savannah tried to move it, but it was too heavy. She rolled on her back in defeat and came face-to-face with Death looking down at her.

There was nothing more she could do. Savannah closed her eyes and waited to die. She would be with her father soon. Only this time, he wouldn't be sick. He wouldn't have those disgusting red eyes anymore. He wouldn't be giving away scary stories for free and scary pass downs. He wouldn't be sick.

Nothing happened. When Savannah opened her eyes, she saw Death holding the ball of gold in its clutch. Death floated over the hole and tossed it back in. The hood looked back over at her and Death pointed at Savannah in warning. It was a matter of seconds before Death turned transparent and disappeared back into the water.

The hot sun and its extreme heat returned. Savannah lay there without a leg, bleeding profusely. She stared up at the sun and didn't close her eyes.

All she could see now was the sun. Savannah closed them and turned her head. When she opened them back up, she came face-to-face with a child's skull.

The Sleepover

By

Joey Beauchamp

For the first time in history, the town of Lancaster, New Hampshire made the front page of the national newspaper. The story was plastered all over the news. After winter break, four mothers had become Angel-Moms.

How could you forget the bodies? How could you forget the blood? How can you forget the violence?

A crowd gathered around outside the house. Police officers created a barrier with yellow tape, their hands outstretched. People were concerned enough to come out of their homes and be out in the frigid cold weather. It was still snowing when they pulled out the bodies of five little girls and one mother. The blood dripped onto the white snow as the black bags were zipped up. The people covered their mouths in horror when they saw the red on the white snow.

Some officers were pushing people out of the way, so paramedics could have a path to get to the girls in time. It was hard to tell which little girl was dead or barely alive. The paramedics arrived with a large ambulance. The red and blue lights shined over the large crowed. They loaded a seven-year-old girl named Ella Thomas into the truck and drove as fast as they could to the Hospital. Snow continued to fall, slowly piling on the streets and onto of the bystanders.

The people gasped as the officers removed a rope around the mother's neck. As the people wept an old lady said in the middle of her prayer, "It was almost Christmas."

What had happened?

*****

Ella watched the snowplow drive in front of her house. It didn't do much good as a pile of snow gathered behind the plow. *"It's so boring here"*, she thought. If she wasn't watching the snow fall, then she would have to play with her dolls, which was only fun for so long. If she wasn't playing with her dolls, then she would be watching reruns of the same cartoon. Ella heard from her mom numerous times "Too much television could fry your brain". What was a little girl supposed to do except watch the snow fall on the roads?

She slumped on the leather couch and let out a big yawn, followed by a sigh.

Ella's mother was in the shower singing Christmas songs. Her mother was excited about the upcoming holiday season and couldn't wait to celebrate. Her mother had a beautiful voice.

Ella got up from the couch and barged into the bathroom, "When will dad be home?"

Her mom's singing was cut short. She then let out a half-assed scream

"Don't scare me like that again," she yelled. Ella's mom pulled the curtain to see Ella standing in the doorway. "Can I have a sleepover?" Ella asked.

"A sleepover on Christmas Eve? I hate to break it to you little girl, but nobody is going to be able to sleep over on Christmas Eve."

"How come?" Ella asked

"What do you mean how come? Its Christmas Eve, the day before Christmas. Everybody is going to doing their own thing with their own families. What don't you understand about that?" Her mom said, annoyed by Ella. She pulled the curtain shut and continued in the shower.

"So, can I have a sleepover?"

"Sweetie . . . I don't care. Your dad is snowed in at the airport and might not be home until tomorrow. If you can get your friends to come over, then you can have the sleepover." Ella ran into the living room in excitement. She knew who she would call first.

*****

Ashley was Ella's best friend. She would tell her friends that they are all her best friends. However, if Ella had to choose only one of them, it would be Ashley. They both had blonde hair and have the same birth month, yet Ashley was a year older. They both liked board games and telling each-other scary stories. They would often gossip about the boys in their class sometimes resulting separation during class.

The phone rang twice before it was picked up by Ashley's mother. Ella didn't acknowledge Ashley's mom.

"Can Ashley spend the night?" asked Ella.

Before Ashley's mom could respond, Ella heard Ashley in the background screaming in excitement. *"Yes! Please mom! I'll do anything!"*

Ella listened closely, as her mother had a small argument with her daughter. Ashley's mother must have put her hand over the receiver so Ella couldn't hear. *"There isn't anything to do in this town . . . we did the same thing last year . . . and the year before that . . . I'll do anything!"*

For a moment, Ella couldn't hear anything on the other end. She pressed the receiver hard into the side of her head so she could hear any sort of feedback.

"I'll be over in an hour." said Ashely. The phone hung up immediately afterward.

*****

Ella had some trouble trying to get Victoria to come over. Victoria was a third grader but grew up with Ella. She had always been around Ella since before she was in school. They had both went to the same church and same daycare. Her mother was a Hispanic lady who did not speak much English.

Victoria answered on the first ring then instructed Ella to wait. Ella stayed on the phone waiting as she heard her and her mother speaking in Spanish. Victoria began to giggle.

"What did you tell your mom?" asked Ella.

"I told her that I was working on a project and it can't wait, and she believed   me."

*****

"It's going to be a wonderful Christmas eve", thought Ella. She ran to her mother and told her who was coming over.

"Ashley and Victoria are coming over in an hour." said Ella.

"An hour?" asked Ella's mom in disbelief. "They better get over here sooner than that, otherwise, their parents will have to spend the night too. The roads are horrible, Ella. They may not make it, so don't get your hopes up."

Her mother turned on the blow dryer and began drying her hair. After about thirty minutes, there was a ring from the doorbell, which interrupted Ella's thoughts.

"Who could that be?" asked Ella's mom. Ella assumed it was her friends but knew they wouldn't make it there that fast.

*****

Ella's mom grabbed the doorknob, but before she turned it, she glanced at Ella. She looked like she'd seen a spider.

"I thought you said your friends were going to be here in an hour?"

"I did, mamma."

She opened the door and came face-to-face with Ms. Calypso and her two daughters, Michelle and Gina.

"Hey girls! Hey Ms. Calypso," she said, smoothly. "Come in and get out of the cold."

The small family walked in and closed the door. Cold followed the family in the warm house. Ms. Calypso kept her hand on the doorknob while she spoke. "Evening neighbor, I really have to drive to Manchester for something urgent. My father is having open heart surgery. Would you mind watching Michelle and Gina till tomorrow?" I am deathly afraid of the roads and if anything happens to me, I want them to at least be safe. I will gladly pay you for your troubles.

There really isn't anything Ella's mom could do. She didn't want to say no and risk offending her. The truth was, Ella's mom was afraid of Ms. Calypso. There were rumors around town, that she was involved with voodoo, witchcraft and the occult. Some have said she worshipped Satan. She would often wear a inverted crucifix necklace under her shirt. Ms. Calypso was an African American woman whose entire family was from Louisiana and the Caribbean. Ella's mother knew that the rumors could be a result in racial stereotypes, but she kept her guard up.

The rumors continued to say that her daughters were the result of a spell or human sacrifice. Ella's mom nor the town had never seen the children's father.

Would it be considered a hate crime, if she told her no and made her walk back in the deep snow? Ella's mother thought to herself. It's like she did this on purpose. Inviting them in was part of her plan all along. She thought as more and more accusations passed through her brain.

"Please Miss Thomas" asked Ms. Calypso. Her voice was low and raspy. One of her eyes was completely white and her teeth were yellow.

Michelle was nine and Gina was thirteen years old. Neither one of them resembled their mother. Ms. Calypso looked older. Really old in fact. She looked as if she was at least seventy. Her hair was in dreadlocks and bundled in a black scarf behind her head. Jewelry adorned nearly every inch of her body. The two girls looked around the house and became excited when they saw Ella pop her head out from behind the couch. "Alright Ms. Calypso," said Ella's mom. "Do they have anything for the night?"

A large torn bag came from behind Ms. Calypso's back and it slammed at the feet of Ella's mom. "Thank you so much Miss Thomas" she said enthusiastically. "I'll be back in the morning for you two. You'll be in good hands. Isn't that right?"

"They'll be just fine." said Ella's mom.

Ms. Calypso gave the girls a kiss on their foreheads and ran into the snow. Her car sped of quickly as if she was an a great hurry.

*****

Ella didn't know Michelle or Gina very well. They went to the same school, yet she avoided them just as everyone else did. It was not about race so much as it was about the girl's odd behavior. The two girls would often try and separate themselves and would purposely eat at different tables than the rest. When people tried to befriend them, they would push them away occasionally demeaning the good intentioned child. She heard that their mom was involved with voodoo and Satanism and used a black magic to conjure her daughters into existence.

They were even dubbed the "Daughters-of-Darkness" at school.

Before Ella could say anything to them, there was a knock at the door. It was Ashley, who dropped her sleeping bag when she saw Michelle and Gina.

"Hiya," said Ashley, awkwardly. "Ella, why are they here?" Ashley was covered in snow, head-to-toe, except her face. Her cheeks were rosy red and wind burned. Ella came over and gave her friend a big hug. "I'm glad you were able to make it early. My mom said the roads are bad."

"They are," said Ashley. "My mom already left so she could get home before the roads get really bad." The girls talked for awhile ignoring Michelle and Gina.

*****

Victoria showed up shortly after Ashley, and she too stepped back when she saw Ms. Calypso's daughters. "oh dios mio," said Victoria. The girls stared at the Michelle and Gina unaware of their disrespect. Ella's mom called for pizza, something the family had done every Christmas eve as tradition. It arrived nearly two hours later and tasted like it had been in the fridge for hours. They ate the pizza and quickly retired to Ella's room.

When the girls were in Ella's bedroom, they pushed all the furniture to the sides of the room. Sleeping bags were sprawled out, giving each girl barely enough room to slide a quarter through. Then then set up a small pink tent near the closet.

Ella, Ashley, and Victoria made sure they weren't close to Michelle and Gina and stared at them awkwardly. It must have been awkward and unwelcoming for the two sisters. Nonetheless they tried to be involved with the girls childlike antics.

Ella's mom told them to go to bed early, so Santa could wrap presents and leave them under the tree. "When you girls go home tomorrow you will get your own presents" Ella's mom reiterated to the rest of the girls.

The moonlight and Christmas lights shone through the side of the tent, giving mild lighting for the girls to see. It wasn't enough, so the girls took out their flashlights and shined them in front of their faces, so they could see each-other talking.

Victoria broke the silence, "Does anybody know any ghost stories?" Ashley and Ella shook their heads, while Michelle and Gina continued to stare. "Vance at school said that he played Charlie Charlie one time." Ashley said.

"He told me that too, right before we broke for winter break," said Ella. "He was also spreading rumors about how he called *Bloody Mary* in the mirror."

To this, all the girls laughed and then it got quiet again when sisters began to stare again.

This time, Ashley broke the silence, "my cousin told me that he once played *Ouija Board* in the Lancaster Cemetery and he's still alive."

"*Let's play Light as A Feather Stiff As A Board*," suggested Ella. "It's easy. I'll lay down and you four chant and try to lift me with just your pointer and middle finger."

Before she could get a response, Ella laid down in the middle of the other girls and crossed her arms over her chest like a bat. The girls looked at one another and agreed to partake in the game. They placed their fingers under Ella and did their chant. Ella did not move an inch. Nobody was surprised.

"This is stupid," said Ashley. She rolled her eyes and crossed her arms.

"Do you guys know what *Brujas* are?" Victoria asked the two sisters. She knew if she asked this question, she could squash the rumors. *Are Michelle and Gina really the Daughters-of -Darkness?*

"What are Bru . . . Bru . . . Brujas?" asked Ella.

"They're witches," said Victoria, smiling. Her plan worked. "Witches that cast spells and fly on broom sticks."

Michelle and Gina both raised their eyebrows and smiled wide. Their smiles gave the girls the creeps. The three girls got close to each other so they could feel safe and remained quiet.

"Our mother isn't a Bruja," said Gina. "We've heard the rumors and they aren't true."

"She's just a little weird," said Michelle.

There was an awkward pause. When Gina spoke again, it made the three girls scream. "There's nothing to be afraid of. Our mother isn't a witch . . . or at least I don't think she is. Is she Michelle?"

She shrugged her shoulders. "Sometimes I hear her talking to herself in the mirror I guess."

"Yeah That is weird?" said Ashley.

"I saw her one day talking to the mirror," continued Michelle. "One time I saw her poke her thumb with a needle then draw a star around her reflection with her blood. When she was done, I heard her say some weird words." "I remember you telling me that," interrupted Gina. "You got in so much trouble for eavesdropping, that she sewed your mouth shut until it was time for dinner."

"What happed to the blood?" asked Victoria.

The Calypso sisters nodded at the same time. Gina finished the rest of the story. "Michelle told me that the bathroom lit up dark red and a dark portal opened. She then heard a man's voice coming from within the portal. "It sounded really low. Like the devil". The girls continued with their story.

*****

"Merry Christmas!" The girls screamed loud and jumped up nearly out of the tent. Ella's mom peeked her head into the tent and said, "Merry Christmas" as loud as she could, and she laughed when all the girls jumped. "You kids need to go to sleep. I can hear you all the way down the hall and you're going to scare away Santa's reindeer."

She stopped laughing when she could see that Ella was glaring at her. The girls then continued playing with toys and telling stories.

*****

Victoria had to go to the bathroom before she went to bed. She walked to the bathroom down the dark hall. She noticed Ella's mom was in her bedroom with the door shut. Victoria still was convinced that Michelle and Gina's mom was in fact a Witch.

She heard kids talking about the sort of black magic Ms. Calypso used. They called it Blood Magic since she used blood to create the portal. Victoria closed the door and looked into the mirror.

Is it possible? Thought Victoria.

After she was done using the toilet, she washed her hands and stared into the mirror. Victoria said Bloody Mary two times instead of three and laughed to herself. She said Candyman four times and laughed again.

There was a cut on her leg from falling on the ice a few days ago. The sharp edges of the ice felt like they could have torn her leg off. Instead it just left her with a giant hole in the side of her calf. It was healing well, but she thought if she picked at it, she could use that blood to draw the star on the mirror. She wouldn't have to bite her thumb or poke her finger.

She grabbed the side of the scab and pulled off a small piece. Blood began to fall down her leg. Victoria then wiped a small piece on his finger tip then placed a wadded-up toilet paper piece to stop the blood. She looked at her reflection and drew a star on the mirror. "Bloody Marry, Bloody Marry Bloody Marry" she said.

*****

Victoria watched the mirror open and a black hole into a dark void opened. She didn't scream from the sheer amazement, but she almost fell backwards. She opened his eyes and mouth wide. *What on Earth is this?*

Cold air was coming into the bathroom and the lights started to flicker on and off. The force from the portal began to pull Victoria. Hands came out form the sinister hole and grabbed a hold of Victoria by the throat. The hands squeezed and didn't soften its grip.

Sharp nails were attached to them and they dug themselves into the back of her neck. Victoria could not move or scream. She was paralyzed by the beast that came from the dark portal. She finally saw its face and its other hand come out of the space in the mirror. It glared with black eyes and iron teeth. An evil grin was on the demon's face and it spoke to her in a low inhuman voice, *"I am Darkness."*

*****

Ella's mom was wrapping the last Christmas present. It was a Princess Tina Doll. Something Ella had wanted for many months but was too expensive to buy. Very carefully, Ella's mom wrapped up Princess Tina.

There was a huge thud sound that made Ella's mom jump and drop the doll. *What was that?* She thought. Princess Tina's face was cracked down the middle and the box was ruined.

What was she going to tell Ella? Tell her that Santa was a little rough with her present?

She walked over to the bedroom door to investigate the sound and when she turned the knob, the door didn't open. It took Ella's mom by surprise when her door was locked and there was no lock on the door. Could it be that her daughter and her friends were playing a practical joke with her? If she wasn't careful, the girls would see the gifts.

"What was that noise?" she asked. This time, she put Princess Tina under her arm and tried with both hands to open the door, but still it didn't budge. It felt like the door was bolted shut. She gave up and pounded her fists on Ella's bedroom door. When there was no answer, she exhaled and leaned against the door in defeat. "Girls, what are you doing in there!?" She yelled.

Just then the door opened by itself and pushed Ella's mom backward. She thought it was the girls, giving up on their game of pulling on the door. "Locking your mother out and scaring her like that isn't very nice Ella" She said, angrily.

It wasn't her daughter or her friends that were holding the door closed. She pushed open the door to reveal a dark room. A dark figure emerged from the closet coming dace to face with Ella's mother. He was a pale bald man with black eyes. He stared at her with an evil look. The "Good evening," Sweat poured from her forehead as she trembled in fear. "Who are you?" She said. The figure then got closer to her face. Ella's mother closed her eyes to avoid eye contact with the figure. "I am Beelzebub". He said.

Before she could utter out a cry for help, something wrapped around her neck and began hoisting her upward. She was dangling from the ceiling and kicking her feet. Princess Tina fell from her arms and broke completely on the floor. She was in an alternate reality. As the life fell from her, she saw the girls in the room playing. Her screams could not be heard, she was invisible to them. The beast pulled Ella's mother down the hallway.

*****

Victoria is taking a long time to go to the bathroom, thought Ella. All four girls were zipped up in their sleeping bags and staring up at the top of the tent. They could see the Christmas lights shining around the window. The moon was bright and when it reflected off the snow, it made the light brighter. It reminded the girls of a white box. It was blurry from the veil of the tent.

Michelle and Gina's story of their mother stuck in her head. Ashley was thinking of it too. They both held each other's hands in fear. Victoria was taking a long time in the bathroom.

There was a loud sound. It sounded like a thud and it scared the girls upright. They all looked in a different direction, trying to figure out where that God awful sound came from.

"What was that?" asked Ashley. Her eyes were wide.

"Shhhhhhh!" said Ella. "Be quiet."

There was the thud sound and then there was the sound of a struggle down the hallway. It was making the wood from the ceiling creak. Like a swing, when you're swinging high.

The girls were frozen in place. They didn't realize it at first, but they were holding their breaths. When they exhaled, they could see their breath. Someone opened the window and let in all the cold air. All at once they saw the shadow. It was inside the white box.

*****

"Let's play a game Girls," said the shadow. Ashley was the first to scream. The shadow poked the side of the tent and cut open an entrance, revealing itself. The demon smiled with his sharp teeth. The beast was human in figure, but the smile was something unworldly. There was a hunger in those black eyes, and they were the last thing Ashley saw before she was ripped from the tent by her leg.

She was thrown through the window and bashed her head on the way out. Blood rained on the snow from the cut on her head. When her body hit the snow, it snuffed out her scream. Ashley took one last breath as the demon threw a glass shard at her head. Michelle and Gina whimpered in fear and couldn't move. Ella quickly scurried past them and ran out the front of the tent. She could hear the Calypso girls screaming in pain and making death noises as she ran towards the front door.

When she opened the door. Snow caved in and fell on top of her. It knocked her on her back and buried her body except for her head. The snow was crushing her, making it hard for her to cry for help. Only a little air was getting through to her lungs. The weight of the snow was slowly killing her.

There was sounds of footsteps coming towards her. They stomped hard on the wooden floor. The demon laughed at the sight of her. His teeth made clicking sounds every time it breathed. Its eyes looked like two black pearls.

*****

The ambulance drove as fast as it could to the Lancaster hospital. Ella's head rocked back and forth, every time the ambulance hit some tall snow and ice. The paramedics were hooking her up to machines and poking her with needles.

They too were just as shocked to see all those girls in that state. The paramedic put a tube down Ella's throat and pumped her lungs full of air. He watched the monitor like a hawk as he did. The other paramedic checked her pulse and took a small flashlight from his pocket.

He turned it on and lifted open Ella's eyelid. "I think she's sick."

"She's not sick, she's dying." said the paramedic whom was pumping the air.

"Her   eyes   are   dark   black!"

The Emerald Child

By

Jorge Harrington

The sounds of gunfire broke through the desert air. Bullets peppered a wooden door, trying to kill the person behind it with no success. The gunfire belonged to large creatures clothed in black robes and golden headdresses. There were two dozen of them trying to complete their task given to them by their master.

Some carried clubs and a few wielded swords. They waited behind the others who were blasting their pistols and shotguns. They screamed a battle cry at the top of their lungs.

A man named Castor was holding his position behind the door. Every few minutes he would return fire to the golden demons. He cursed them and their master while he reloaded his guns.

"You golden vermin! The lot of you!" Castor emptied his magazine through a hole in the door and finally struck one in the shoulder. The sound the creature let out could spoil milk.

When he went to reach for ammo in his side purse, he found that there wasn't enough ammo for them all. If he didn't shoot back, the cloaked figures would know that he was empty and would swarm him.

The small house he was in had a giant hole in it. Thank goodness the creatures didn't notice it, otherwise the ones with the swords would be able to flank him. Caster looked out of a hole and saw the creatures throwing rocks at the building, trying to weaken the door. The door was going to give way any second.

He shot one bullet to every ten they shot at him. Soon he was left with four shots. Just then he felt a tug on his pant leg and with a sudden move he had a pistol shoved under his chin.

"Take it easy partner, it's only me," said Inquisitor Telemon. "I knew if I followed the sounds of killing I would find you."

"Where's the robot?"

"Who? TAO-38? I don't know. He was supposed to be opening up that metal door a few blocks over. I told him that I was going to get you . . ."

"Are you ever going to shut up?" said Caster, cutting off Telemon. He grabbed the ammo purse that was around Telemon's waist. He too was carrying guns on his sides and a short sword was in its scabbard.

Before Caster could tell Telemon that the robot better have the door open soon. A club had crashed through the door, bringing in the first cloaked figure. Castor and Telemon both fell over backwards, dumping their bag of ammo all over the floor.

Telemon quickly recovered and pulled out his sword. He dodged another swing of the club and was able to cut the side of the vermin. It didn't do much to stop another swing at him, but Telemon was a small man and that was making him a harder target to hit.

Three cloaked swordsmen came in and focused on Castor who picked up his hat from the dirt. He shot one in the gut and ducked in time to save the marriage between his head and his shoulders. This would be one of many times during this attack that he came close to death.

Fear was trying to creep into Castor's mind. That was what these creatures did. They drove fear into the hearts of men with every appearance and stroke of their weapons. Doubt in oneself killed a man when dealing with demons like these.

The creature that Telemon was wrestling with had finally made a wrong move and was dealt a killing blow to the neck. When one cloaked figure fell, another took its place. The cloaked swordsman had taken a frustrated swing at Caster only to miss again and chopped off his partner's head. The body crashed to the floor like a puppet with its strings cut.

This may have been avoided if Caster didn't sneak into the black castle and steal the master's treasure. The Emerald Child.

The Garden

By

Joey Beauchamp

The smell of cigarette smoke came wafting in from the outside. It always did. Every day for six years it smelled like a nasty campfire. Kent was sitting at the kitchen table of his small one-bedroom apartment, reading a real estate magazine. His apartment was a studio barely big enough to fit him and his fiancé who was eight months pregnant.

"Our baby isn't going to live very long with all of your friends smoking all the time," said Jessica.

"They're not my friends," he said. "They're the neighbors."

She hoped that if she poked him enough, he would get the hint. "What would happen if our baby comes out with black lungs?"

Kent tried to ignore her. "Let me finish this article first and I'll go out and talk to them." Kent just wanted to finish his magazine.

She came over and lifted her shirt up and pushed Kent's magazine out of the way with her pregnant belly. Kent let the magazine drop to the floor. He looked at his fiancés belly then back up at her. He wondered how on Earth, can a living person, have the energy to constantly nag him. "Go out there and tell our neighbors that they're going to kill themselves and kill our baby at the same time."

Before Kent could utter a word in defense, she stormed away from his area and sat on a couch.

*****

Kent had three neighbors and all four of them shared the same fence in the backyard. All three of them smoked like constantly. It was a social thing for the friends. Every time one of them laughed, smoke would seep out of their mouth. They smelled like ash that came from the end of the cigarette. Just a bunch of average Joes. Left to right, their names were Jonathan, Robert, and Jake.

Jonathan worked at the local grocery store and took up smoking a year after he had been married. Robert delivered newspapers during graveyard hours and was going through a divorce. Robert had smoked cigarettes since he was twelve.

Jake was sixty-six years old and was taking care of his dying wife. Leukemia was slowly winning the battle. Jake looked healthy, ironically. Technically should have been him with the cancer and laying in his death bed.

"Look who decided to join us," said Robert. He blew a smoke ring at Kent, who just waved it away. Kent then stuck his hands in his pockets awkwardly.

"I saw your girlfriend the other day at the grocery store with her mom," said Jonathan. "I can't believe you got with a nineteen-year-old-blondie. You're a real pervert, Kent."

Kent's face immediately began to turn bright red. It was hard to tell if it was him being self-conscience, or from all of the smoke.

"Isn't she almost due?" asked Jake. He leaned on his hands, over the fence, as his cigarette smoke disappeared near Kent's apartment.

Robert's eyes opened wide, when he heard that she was pregnant. "Are you kidding me? She's nineteen! How come I didn't hear about this?"

"You work graveyard," said Kent. Trying to hold his breath.

"So, what was she? A one-night-stand?" asked Jake.

"It was an accident," said Kent. He looked over his shoulder to make sure Jessica wasn't eavesdropping.

"You've ruined her life," said Jonathan, jokingly. Smoke came out of his nose while he laughed at his joke. The other two neighbors smiled at each other and at Jonathan's poke at Kent.

"I didn't have a condom and I didn't know when I was ever going to get with a "ten" again. I'm thirty-six years old. People think I'm her dad and you should see the look they give me when they see she's pregnant".

They all started laughing again. Jake pushed his cigarette butt into the fence and immediatly lit another one up. He started talking as soon as the laughing stopped. "If you're going to have a family with her, you're going to need a bigger place to live."

Jonathan nodded. "It's hardly big enough to fit me and my wife in."

"It was the amount of space in the apartment that killed my relationship," said Robert. He took a huge drag on his cigarette.

It took all of Kent's might to tell them what he really was thinking. "I am moving out."

All three of them blew their smoke out and it engulfed Kent's face.

"Was it anything that we did?" asked Jake.

"It's our smoking that is killing his relationship," answered Robert, who lit another cigarette.

"How come you didn't tell us sooner?" asked Jonathan.

Kent's face turned red again and then he started to panic when he looked over his shoulder and saw Jessica staring at them. The look on her face could stop anyone in their tracks. "We're moving because you guys don't know when to quit. Constantly smoking and shit"

Kent feared that if he didn't do the right thing, he would go to some sort of Hell with fire, and brimstone. He thought that if he didn't do what Jessica wanted, he would be tortured in the depths of his own Hell.

"Jonathan let the cigarette fall out of his mouth. It dangled by the butt on the edge of his lips. He looked as though he was betrayed.

Jake shook his head and flicked his lit cigarette at Kent like a used toothpick. "Shame on you."

"I'm sorry, I didn't mean it like that-"

"We all heard what you said," said Robert. "A little honesty didn't kill anyone. Grow a backbone while you're gone."

*****

"What did you tell your friends?" asked Jessica. She opened the door for Kent as he walked in with his head down and his shoulders hunched. He sat at the kitchen table and grabbed the phone off the receiver.

He grabbed the magazine he was reading and flipped threw the pages. He wanted to avoid any conversation with his wife. He flipped to a page that had a picture of a man in a pink bow-tie and a pointy mustache.

She poked her belly into his face causing him to drop the phone and the magazine. "I said, did you tell your friends about how their smoke is killing my baby?"

Kent stared at Jessica's giant belly. She thought it looked cute. He just shook his head and picked up the phone. "I told them that we're moving."

"No, you didn't," she said. Her eyebrow was raised. "It looked like you were out there having a good with your friends."

"We weren't being friendly," Kent protested. He reached down and picked up the phone and the magazine from the floor. "I said we're moving. I'm trying to call this real estate agent."

Jessica was so excited, that she jumped in his lap and hugged him tightly. Kent could feel the her belly button poking into his chest. The phone and the magazine dropped to the floor again. "I was right about you."

"What were you right about?"

"That you always do the right thing."

*****

"Hello?" Kent was standing in the corner with the receiver up to his ear. He couldn't concentrate on what he was going to say and answer all of Jessica's questions at the same time. He looked away from her and had a tiny fraction of privacy.

"Who are you talking to? How much is it going to cost? Will we live closer to my parents or yours when the baby comes."

"Thanks for calling, Mr. Wednesday's Real Estate, I'm Mr. Wednesday and I'd be happy to show you the house of your dreams." The questions poured out like lava-flow.

Kent thought Mr. Wednesday sounded like some sort of cartoon character. *Who wears a pink bow tie? Bill Nye?* "I'm looking to buy a house."

"You've done the right thing by calling me bud". The man on the other end answered

Did he just call me bud? Thought Kent. "When can I earn your business?" The man said. Kent did not know the first thing about buying a house. He tried to sound as smart as possible "I'm interested in purchasing an establishment"

Mr. Wednesday let out a harsh cackling laugh. "I never heard of anybody who said it quite like that. I can meet Today at seven-thirty or tomorrow at eight-thirty, PM. I'm so delighted."

"Ask him if he has any openings today," said Jessica, enthusiastically. Kent could feel Jessica's belly button poking into his back, while she tried to get closer and hear the conversation. Suddenly, the corner became catastrophic.

"Do you happen to have a spouse?"

"Yes sir," said Kent. He put up a finger to signal Jessica to be quiet while he was on the phone.

"Are you two expecting?"

"We are, kind of weird how you know that" said Kent."

"Don't be rude to him," said Jessica. She gave Kent a violent nudge.

"I didn't mean to pry. I'm excited to meet you guys today and will gladly show you your new home." Kent pressed END on the receiver and it made a loud beep noise. "What did he say?" she's said, sounding even more enthusiastic than before. "We meet him tonight".

*****

Kent didn't remember telling Mr. Wednesday his address. When eight-thirty rolled around. There was a buzz at the door. Kent opened the front door. There stood Mr. Wednesday. He looked different from his pictures. A tall, lanky, man with a face that looked like he had been through quite a lot. "Yes", Kent said. "You're that man Kent was talking to. The Real Estate Agent."

"Right you are little miss, right you are. I'm here for both of you, I am Mr. Wednesday. "Oh Mr. Wednesday!" Kent said surprised to see a slightly different looking man than the advertisement. He pulled Jessica away from the door like she was in danger.

She escaped Kent's hold on her shoulders. Jessica and Kent looked at Mr. Wednesday for a few seconds. Jessica looked at the man and thought his pink bow-tie was a bit strange. Kent thought of something entirely different. He wondered how this man knew so much about him, when he told him so little. Or did he forget that he told him? He couldn't think straight with Jessica asking so many questions coupled with the smell of the neighbor's smoke-filled area.

"You must be Kent Brady?" asked Mr. Wednesday. He offered his hand to Jessica. "and you must be?"

She looked at his pink bow-tie and then at his grin. It was almost cartoonish. "Jessica Hallwell, but soon to be Mrs. Kent Brady."

Mr. Wednesday looked at the ring that was on Jessica's finger. She flashed it at him like she was the happiest person in the world. "Ain't that something? I don't mean to be rude or anything, but you look really young."

"Well thank you! I'm old enough to do what I want," said Jessica. She looked at Kent and smiled big. "I love him so much. We're going to buy our forever house."

"Is that true, Kent Brady?"

He nodded and couldn't believe what he was doing. It felt like all of this was happening too fast. He was about to buy a house from a guy named after one of the days of the week. His nineteen-year-old fiancé was eight months pregnant with his first child. The neighbors shunned him and he was almost old enough to be Jessica's father. Was he doing the right thing?

An elbow was delivered into the ribs of Kent, which made him wince in pain. "He's talking to you. Pay attention!"

"Where do we begin?" asked Kent. Mr. Wednesday pulled out a pen and notepad.

"May I ask why you're purchasing a house?" asked Mr. Wednesday. "We want a bigger place. Our family is growing" Kent answered. "May I take you to a couple?" Wednesday said enthusiastically. It was early in the morning, but they knew this was the only time they could both look at houses together.

He drove Kent and Jessica to three houses. All of them would suffice, but Jessica wasn't feeling it. Each time she changed her mind on a house, Mr. Wednesday would take them to a more expensive house. "here's a beautiful four bedroom" he would say. His sales pitch began to get stale.

"Listen, this is going to be our forever house. We want it perfect," said Jessica. She had Kent's arm around her and his other hand, pinned to the top of her belly. Kent felt their baby move.

"Is that true, Kent?"

Kent watched his words carefully. He didn't want to upset anyone, so he agreed Jessica. He thought it was odd. Sitting in the middle of the backseat, instead of sitting in the front seat with somebody he was negotiating with.

He nodded.

"Alright then, I have one more house to show you. It's a little out of the way, but it'll be a wonderful forever house for you. You'll be doing your baby a great favor if you buy this house."

Mr. Wednesday's car was a white mustang, with pink interior and fur walls. It was cartoonish, like Mr. Wednesday. Kent felt like he was going to pass out from boredom He then saw the smile on Jessica's face, he knew he had to swallow his pride and insecurities. It wouldn't do anybody good, if he started spouting off how he really felt about the whole situation.

*****

The drive felt comfortable and peaceful, until they left town. By now it was around noon. An awkward feeling took over them. Each person in the car, started to sweat uncontrollably. Nobody said a thing about it. The color of the day seemed to have a blue veil over it, but the sun shined down hard on the car. Soon the town began to disappear in the rear-view-mirror.

Tumbleweeds and dust-devils were swirling around each other. Mr. Wednesday took a handkerchief out of his front pocket and dabbed his forehead. "I promise, when you see it. You'll love everything about it."

"Tell us about it Mr. Wednesday," asked Jessica. She kissed Kent on the cheek and gave him a smile.

"The previous owners were scientists. They studied plants or flowers, something like that."

"You mean Botanist?" asked Kent in a snarky tone.

"Yeah, anyways, they up and left the house and nobody has seen them since. They left it vacant for years, but with my help and money, I was able to restore it to its former self.". Mr. Wednesday said, pushing the sale. "That's not creepy at all" Kent said snarky.

"Can you see that big yellow house?"

Kent and Jessica saw Mr. Wednesday, pointing to a house on a hill. They couldn't believe their eyes. A large Victorian style mansion lay in the distance.

*****

The car turned toward the direction of a rocky path. It was as if it was forgotten in time. Trees with pink and yellow leaves made a path to the house. There were no houses on either side of the street and the sidewalk was cracked. Broken cement blocks plagued it, making it unwalkable. It seemed as though the house was laying in its own neighborhood, cut off from the entire city.

Kent and Jessica only noticed it, because Mr. Wednesday pointed it out to them. "It just needs a little bit of paint and it'll look like it just came out of a Better Homes magazine."

"This place a mansion "Jessica said. She rubbed her belly and recounted all the windows.

Mr. Wednesday pulled out a ring of keys from his pocket and found a small shiny silver key. He then opened the lock on the giant door. "It's been transformed into a mansion after I purchased it. It was used as a laboratory by the previous owners."

Kent heard the metal ping from the lock, indicating that Mr. Wednesday's key had worked.

"Eight bedrooms, four bathrooms, "said Mr. Wednesday, as they entered the house. Mr. Wednesday turned the light on.

Before they went into the house, something caught his eye. There were a bunch of crows flying around in a circle.

"Is there a giant nest of crows on top of the roof?" asked Kent.

"That's what gives this house it's soul," Mr. Wednesday answered. "They eat from the garden."

*****

"A garden?" asked Jessica. She squeezed Kent's arm in excitement. "Inside the house?"

"Inside the house Soon-to-be-Mrs. Brady, you're correct. I think you got a keeper." Mr. Wednesday answered. They were standing in the middle of the living room and couldn't believe how huge it was inside. Sun beamed into the windows and onto the classic wooden floors.

It was dark and quiet. There was something mysterious about the house, but Kent couldn't put his finger on it. He didn't feel good since his outburst with his neighbors. The living room they were standing in, was bigger than their apartment. Any sign of anxiety he was feeling, was stomped out of existence, because he knew buying a house would be the right thing to do.

"The garden is in this next room," said Mr. Wednesday. He pointed to a much larger door, that was down a massive hall with a large crystal chandelier. "Shall I show it to you?"

Kent's eyes widened. How could a garden be inside of the house? He looked at Jessica, who just batted her eyes at him.

Mr. Wednesday began to lead us towards the garden door. It was the only door that was painted a forest green color. The rest of the doors were brown. He talked as he walked and pointed at things in the house. The closer they got to the door, the more he talked about it. When the door was opened it revealed a large greenhouse within the house itself. A greenhouse about fifty feet by fifty feet. Sun shined through the glass ceiling.

Everything in the garden was untouched. There were a lot of plants and colors in there that he had never seen before. "So, my team and I repaired the house and remolded it in a way so the garden could live inside the house. It runs itself, which means you never have to water it yourself, and you don't have to open any windows to let in sunlight."

There was something off about the greenhouse. Something Kent could not quite put his finger on. Although the greenhouse was beautifully lit, it felt dark and foreboding. The kind that gave you an uneasy feeling.

It felt like Willy Wonka and the Chocolate Factory, when they entered the garden. Only there was nothing eatable and the water was undrinkable. Mr. Wednesday walked to the edge of darkness in the room and stood in the middle of the sunlight. Small shadows of crows were circling, and their "caws" could be heard.

"Isn't it wonderful? "he said, with his hands in the air. "I think they did a great job on the greenhouse. Look around, but please don't touch anything. I have no idea what sort of plants there are, so I would stay far away from them, they could be poisonous."

"I don't have to see them. I can smell them. It smells like wet dirt." Ken said. "That's the manure we recently added to stir the plants".

Jessica was holding her nose tight, "I can smell everything. My allergies are going out of control. I need to step out of the room. Come with me."

"Hold on just sec, I want to see what's over here." Kent walked off in a direction that was farthest away from the door. He was almost to the back of the green house, when he heard running behind him and felt a poke in his back.

"Your baby and I need to leave the room! Please come with me!" screamed Jessica. She grabbed Kent by the arm. To Kent's surprise, she was able to scare him, strong-arm him, and almost made him fall.

As he fell, his hands grabbed a thorny red plant. "Damn it Jessica, I've cut myself." Blood fell into the planter box.

*****

"I'm sorry babe!" screamed Jessica. She sneezed uncontrollably. "If I sneeze hard enough, I can feel our baby coming out, or I might piss myself."

Mr. Wednesday and Kent looked at each-other. It was something that they'll never understand.

"My God! Your hand!" said Jessica. Kent was bleeding nearly uncontrollably. Blood dripped from his palm. She uncrossed her legs and walked over to Kent.

"I'm terribly sorry," said Mr. Wednesday. "I should have told you that there are plants with thorns in there. I will get someone in-"

"We'll take the house." said Jessica. Kent looked at her like she was crazy.

"You have no idea how much it is, and we haven't seen the rest of the house." said Kent, who was looking at his hand. He didn't know if he should be more concerned with his cut, or with Jessica's sudden burst of confidence.

"I'll tell you what," said Mr. Wednesday. "I'll let you stay here for two months, free of charge. I feel bad for you getting hurt and I like you two. I know it's out far from any city or town, but you can raise a family in peace."

"That'll work," said Jessica. "Can you take us back to our apartment so I can get his hand fixed up."

"You guys are doing the right thing. Let me take you home and we'll fill out some paper work."

*****

It had been three weeks since they moved into the house. Kent didn't know how to react. There were no neighbors or strangers to talk to when he went outside. There was no cigarette smoke. There wasn't a lot of stuff to move and with the home-welcoming-party, they didn't have much to fill up the giant house.

Jessica prepared a delicious lunch for the both of them. Instead of sitting at the dining room table, they had a picnic inside one of the empty rooms on the floor. Kent wasn't thrilled about the look on his fiancé's face. She was thinking about changing the rooms again. "Should this be the baby's room"?

It took Jessica a week to choose a room for them and the baby, "we can have the baby sleep with us or have the office turned into a nursery?"

"Master bedroom? All the rooms are master, we just need to pick one. Whatever you choose, dear. My hand is throbbing again." Kent retracted

"Our baby's feet are kicking my kidneys," she complained. "I told you to go get that checked out. It looks bad, even with all the bandages. "Jessica said annoyed at Kent and the baby.

"I did go get it checked out. We went weeks ago. I was going to-"

"You haven't been the same since you cut your hand. You talk in your sleep and sometimes I can hear you talking to yourself."

Kent didn't know what to say. He just ate a cracker and looked out the window.

"Don't run away from me!" she dipped her fingers in some milk and flicked it at Kent. Some of it got on her belly.

"How am I running away?" he crushed up some crackers and blew into his hand. It got all over the picnic.

"I don't know for sure," she said. "You're just not the same. It's like you're looking for someone else."

"That's not true at all," said Kent. He got up and started to walk towards the bedroom door.

"Did I offend you?"

There was no answer from him. He left her there covered in cracker dust.

*****

Kent went outside of the house to clear his head. Jessica was right, he didn't feel himself. He wasn't sure if he was doing the right thing. Living all the way out in the middle of nowhere? Being stuck in some large house with his pregnant girl?

He looked up and saw the bright large moon. Was it night time already? Did they really have a picnic that lasted all day?

"Did you do it yet?" A dark ominous voice cried out.

"Who said that?" he said. The voice sounded eerie like a combination of his friends.

"You forgot us already? Shame on you!" the voice said again.

"Robert?" Kent rubbed his eyes and squinted in the dark.

"A one-night stand, turned into a lifetime."

"Stop it!"

The darkness started to lighten up with the moons light. Now, it was only focused in one spot. Kent could see the silhouette of three men standing behind a fence and smoke protruding out of their mouths and covering their face.

"We're only trying to help!" said the voice. *"You're old like me. That baby is going to kill you."*

"Kids ruin marriages," said Robert's voice. *"Believe me! I'm the living product of that."*

"My wife isn't much older than Jessica, but I read that marriages fail when you marry them young like that," said Jonathan's voice.

He put his hands to his ears and shook his head hard. So many thoughts were going through Kent's head, he was getting anxiety at a high velocity.

"You can't ignore us. We're your neighbors!"

"I'll help you with the divorce papers in a few months."

"I don't think it's right at all. You are much older than she is."

*****

Kent ran as fast as he could into the house. Jessica saw Kent run past her holding his ears. Kent? She got up from sitting and began chasing him slowly, while holding her belly. Jessica came to one of the hallways. The sound of stomping feet dissipated. She proceeded to walk slowly through the hallway looking into each room. She looked to her left and then to her right.

Going right would lead her towards the front door. To her left, would lead her towards the garden. She chose left and began to search for him. Where could he have gone?

She got closer and closer to the garden door. There was no way she was going to search there first. It would set off her allergies and she would risk sneezing herself into labor. It was her biggest fear while being pregnant.

She heard something move in garden. Jessica stopped a few inches from the door. She hesitated to open the door. The smell of soil and fresh plants seeped their way underneath the doorway. "You think you're so smart don't you?" she said, swinging open the garden door. She'd forgotten how dark it was in there. She pinched her nose, careful to not let the pollen from the plants enter her nose.

She walked until she was in the middle of the room. Once she was in the circle of small sunlight, she couldn't make out the rest of the room. She went to yell but was taken over by sneezing. "Kent? Where did you go?"

Just then a loud thump was heard behind her. Jessica jumped and immediately turned toward the source of the sound. Somebody had shut the garden door on her. The garden room was immediately pitch black. Soon the sun was completely down, and the only light was emitting from the moon. The body emerged from the darkness and it was staring at her. "You scared me!" Kent violently grabbed Jessica. "You're scaring our baby! Where did you go! Ouch! Let go of me! You're hurting me!"

*****

The garden room was quiet. Except for the sounds of Kent shoveling into a hole. It was only two more shovel scoops until it was completely filled up. Then he shoved the shovel into the top of the dirt mound and leaned on the handle.

"You're acting like a man now."
"She was going to leave you anyways."
"Now you don't have anything to worry about."

Kent wiped his brow and let out a sigh of relief. He felt like he was on top of the world. Finally, he would be free. Then he felt two hands land on top of shoulders. It was a woman's hand and a man's hand. Both hands burst through the soil and grabbed a hold of Kent's ankles *"You did the right thing, Kent."*

"Take me home," said Kent. Possessed by some sort of entity. "Take me!"

He yelled the entire time he was slipping deeper into the dirt.

*****

Mr. Wednesday had been trying to call the Brady's for a few days now. He went over what sort of legal action he should take if they were avoiding his calls on purpose. Then he went and did some research to see if he was going to get in trouble if he shows up unannounced.

He decided to drive to the property and see what the family was doing. When he arrived at the house, vines had nearly taken over the entire house. Windows were broken and the front doors paint was chipped

He waited for nearly a half hour outside the home. He knocked a dozen times. Mr. Wednesday used his key and opened the door.

"Kent! Where are you guys?" he called at the top of his lungs, afraid to enter the house. There wasn't a response. Only the sound of dripping water. It sounded like it was moving farther and farther away. "Jessica! Are you not at home?" he walked towards the middle of the house and saw the garden door open. His hand was placed on his pink bow tie in fear. Then he looked down at the floor and saw what was coming out of the dark room.

There were muddy footprints and a drop of blood, leading through the kitchen and up the walls. They were going in all directions. It was the size of the footprints. They were the size of baby   feet.

Shavings

By

Jorge Harrington

"How come you don't ask out the deli girl?" asked Ronald. He poked his coworker in the side with his pointer finger. "She's hot and you need a rebound."

Eli didn't say a word and cut open a case of Spanish Rice to stock the shelf. "I don't want to talk about girls right now. I have the worst luck with girls anyways."

"Come on," said Ronald. "She's new in town and even though she looks emo, I think you two would make a great couple. Just look at her."

He couldn't look at her, because it would remind him of the breakup. Ronald grabbed his arm and jerked him away from the grocery shelf and faced him towards the girl.

Eli saw her and immediately froze. She was leaning on her right hand and tapping the counter with the left.

Her hair was jet black and so was her nail polish. She wore one pigtail on the right side of her head, resembling some sort of anime character.

"Look at the time," said Ronald. He put his hands-on Eli's shoulders and pushed him towards her. "You look like you need a sandwich, Eli. Would you mind making one?"

Eli's face turned bright red in embarrassment. Ronald had said it loud enough that she was able to hear him. Ron chuckled and walked away. She raised her eyebrow in confusion and then looked at Eli.

The silence was deafening. The girl behind the counter started to look like she was going to run away in fear. Eli finally gained the courage to speak and opened his mouth, "May I have a sandwich?"

"What do I look like? Your mother?" she asked.

Eli began to sweat. *What should I say after this?*

"I'm just kidding. What can I get for you? Do you like bologna, Italian, what?"

Bologna, he nodded. *If we were the last people on Earth, she would kill herself before being with me,* he thought.

She wrote the order down on a sticky note and stuck it on the metal shelf, so she could read it. Her clothes covered her arms and her neck, and her eyes were a beautiful blue. Eli could do nothing but stare at her beauty.

"Is that everything for you?" She looked at him and scrunched her eyebrows together.

Once she spoke, Eli snapped out of his daze and shook his head. "I'm sorry. I don't know what just happened. . . um . . . are you new in . . . um . . . town?"

"Today would make five days," she said. "I'm a fast learner. Don't be fooled by me. Even though I just moved here, doesn't mean I know what everyone is up to." She pushed his made sandwich she made in front of him.

His wallet was in his back pocket, but when he went to reach for it. She put her hand up and interrupted him, "Don't worry, It's on me."

"You don't have to do that," said Eli. Her act of kindness made him feel uncomfortable.

"Just because I'm new in town, doesn't mean I don't have any money. You're just going to have to take me out tonight."

"I don't even know your name." his eyes were gigantic.

"My name's Omi."

*****

Eli didn't see Omi for the rest of the day. He told Ronald all the details, "I told you'd find a new girl. No more of that other one."

Now he was in his bathroom, combing his hair. He wanted to impress Omi and he wanted to look sharp doing so. Omi was going to be off work in an hour. She told him that she was going to meet him at La Flama Mexican Restaurant, and not to be late. With the constant anxiety – fueled by the fear of his attire, Eli began to sweat. He thought of what he's going to say to Omi on the date, yet his past breakup was still in the back of his mind.

He thought about his ex all the time and there was nothing he could do. Eli didn't think anyone would like him like that ever again. It hurt for a long time. Every day for six months, his ex was on his mind, but not now. All that was on his mind was the date.

Eli decided on a look that he thought she might like. That was a black t-shirt and blue jeans. He tipped the bottle of cologne into his palm and put it under his armpits, around his neck, and put a drop in the front of his pants.

He bought some red roses at a small gift shop that was next to the Restaurant. The twelve roses were tied together with a dark red ribbon. They looked and felt so delicate, Eli put them in the car and buckled them up in the passenger-seat.

She told him that she got off at six and would be an hour. Eli parked his car in the back of the building and got out of the car. He took a napkin from his backseat and wiped the sweat protruding from his forehead.

His watch read" 7:05 and instantly, is his flight-or-fight system was going awry. He felt light headed when he walked up to the front door. Eli counted to ten and took two deep breaths.

What if she doesn't show up? What if she's already here? Do I kiss her? Do I make a move? Is kissing her making a move?

"There you are!" said a girl's voice through the crack of an ajar metal door. "I got us a booth in the bar section."

Eli jumped in fear startled by Omi's abrupt welcome. Eli closed and opened his eyes trying to calculate what had just happened. To his amazement, Omi was no longer there. He then saw the door then swing shut. *Was that Omi?*

*****

The bar was to the left. If he heard her correctly, she was waiting for him in the bar. Eli had only been twenty-one for only a couple months and had yet to set foot in a bar. When he did, she was sitting in a red booth and she looked like a ghost.

Her face was painted white and her lipstick was dark black. It made Omi's teeth look like they were glowing. Her neck, shoulders, and wrists were exposed. She was covered from head-to-toe in tattoos. Black and gray. No other colors, except for her blue eyes.

Omi resembled a beautiful gothic emo girl. "These are for you," said Eli. Shoving the flowers at her with force. Pedals flew into the air as Omi took hold of Eli's gift.

"Oh . . . thanks? "You . . . um . . . you can sit down."

Eli sat down and quickly picked up a menu.

The waitress came over and Eli could hear her and his date whispering to each-other. Eli looked over the top of his menu and both girls stopped their chatter and looked at him.

"May I take your order?" asked the waitress.

His heart was pounding in his chest. This was the same waitress that waited on him and his ex-girlfriend. What could she be thinking of him?

"What would you like to eat?" he asked Omi. His voice cracked. The waitress tried to hold her laugh back.

"You order first," said Omi. She didn't want to be rude.

"Um . . . I . . . uh . . . would like the chicken tacos, please. Is that okay?"

"We can share," said Omi, helping. She took the menu from Eli and handed it to the waitress. "Thanks."

*****

After she brought them their food and drinks, Omi finally took pity on Eli and spoke to him. "You haven't been on a date in a long time. Am I right?"

He thought this girl must like him, if she was still here after all the silence and awkwardness. Eli nodded and he was red in the face.

"I can tell," she said, smiling. "It's because of your ex?"

Eli's eyes twisted in shape. *How the hell did she know?*

Omi giggled. "Would you believe me if I told you; my previous job I was a fortune teller?" She didn't allow Eli to respond." . I know you don't like to talk about it, because you think about her all the time. You might as well tell me. Give me your hand."

She reached over and took his hand. Eli felt as though his head might explode. He hadn't felt a woman's touch since a good while before the breakup. It made him feel warm and fuzzy inside. Omi was reading his palm.

"Her name is Alexia," she said.

How did she know? Thought Eli. He listened to her while she traced the lines in the middle of his hand.

"She told you something that haunts your dreams. Alexia made the statement, that you've never done anything challenging in your life." Omi didn't have to look at him to know she was right.

"Alexia took you for granted. She used you for your time and your money. If she didn't have it her way, she would shame you into spending money that you didn't have. "Eli tensed up hearing his truth coming from her mouth.

"You think all women are this way. You've been burned and you're going your own way. You blame yourself for everything and take offense when people call you a nice-guy."

Omi let go of his hand, "you can't tell under my mask, but I'm blushing. You were burned by women, but you still asked me out."

"I did?" asked Eli. She put a hand up to this mouth, in disbelief. He didn't remember asking her out, but there is the risk of offending her, so he lied. "I mean, I did. You're the exception." They sat and ate their dinner. Eli opened up slightly to Omi during the date.

"Walk me home, Eli."

"Right now?" he asked.

Omi nodded. She pulled out a twenty-dollar bill and slammed it on the table. "I live at the end of main street."

*****

They walked out of La Flama and down the dark street, towards Omi's house. Eli never walked down this part of town before. Due to the rumors of gangs.

There is a first for everything. First the breakup and now he was looking at the black house that belong to the pale faced girl.

"Beautiful, isn't it?" she said. Both looked up at the house, "most people are afraid of it, but I love it."

"This house?" asked Eli. He couldn't believe what he just said out loud, "I didn't mean it like that. It's just this house has been abandoned for years. Everyone thinks it's haunted."

"That's why I bought it. So far, I haven't seen anything strange. I have something for you. I feel it will help you get over yourself. I call it unworthiness." Omi squeezed Eli's hand and whispered in his ear. She told him to, "wait right here."

Eli twiddled his thumbs and thought to himself. *You're supposed to kiss girls at the end of a date.* If he didn't, how else is she going to know that he likes her.

The sound of Omi's door opening back up, was enough to snap Eli out of his fantasy. She was hiding something behind her back.

Eli came close to Omi and went in for the kiss. Before he could kiss her black lips, she shoved what she had behind her back into his arms. It was a black, rectangular box.

"What's this?"

She avoided his question, "I'll tell you what. You take this home and do what it says on the paper in the box, and I'll have you over for a night you'll never forget." said Omi with a wink.

"I don't understand," he said. The box was heavy in his hands.

"Let me be clear. If you take this home and do what it says on the paper, I'll sleep with you."

Eli grabbed the box.

"Okay, I'll give it a try." Eli grabbed the box without hesitation and smiled awkwardly. Omi then gave him a quick kiss on the cheek and walked back into the house.

*****

Eli was home now. He laid the box on top of his kitchen table and sat on the coach. *Did she really say what I thought she said? She was willing to sleep with him, if he played with whatever was in the box?*

He thought about calling Ronald and telling him about the date and her proposition. Except the box was sticking out like a sore thumb. Eli picked up the box and placed it on the coffee table, in front of him.

It was a simple lock mechanism, which only required Eli to twist the knob and lift the lid open. Inside was a parchment. It read:

Hide and Seek

My name is Shavings and I want to play a game with you. Hide me anywhere you like and count to twenty. After you've counted, come and seek me. Once you found me, it will then be my turn. Place me in the corner and you hide. When I get to twenty . . .

There was nothing more. Eli thought that was odd . . .

*****

He reached inside the box and pulled out a small wooden marionette puppet, about two feet in length. It had no strings attached to him. "This must be the doll named Shavings?" Eli said out loud.

Eli was able to stand him up on the coffee table and have look at him. He was a hunter, with a quiver full of arrows and a bow. They were carved right onto his body. Shavings beard was red and thick. He looked as if he was a mountain man. It made Eli think of Robin Hood, only this version of him was creepier.

Was Omi really going to have sex with him if he played Hide and Seek with this puppet? Was it worth it? This sort of deal was better than the deal he got with his ex. The deal of a near sexless relationship.

There was no avoiding the feeling of stupidity, as he picked Shavings up by the arm and looked for a hiding spot. His house had only two bedrooms and a tiny bathroom.

In the spare bedroom was where Eli decided to hide him. *Under the bed! No that would be too easy. How about, on top of a shelf? No that's stupid too.*

A trunk was at the end of the bed. That would be a good place to hide Shavings. It was empty and would be easy to find him when Eli went to go look for him.

The whole situation was strange and awkward. How would Omi know if he played with the doll? Eli thought to himself.

While Eli was placing Shavings in the trunk. He accidentally let him slip from his fingers, because how awkwardly heavy he was. On the way down, something cut Eli's finger wide open.

*****

Along with Shavings bow and arrows, there was a small sword hidden under the sleeve of his right arm.

"You tricky bugger!" he said, putting his opened wound in his mouth and letting the lid shut tight.

The first aid kit was in the bathroom. That puppet's blade was razor sharp. It didn't take much to cut into his fingers. He was surprised how deep it was. It took him fifteen minutes to clean the wound and dress it up.

It was what Omi promised him that kept him playing this game. It sounded too good to be true, but it's been such a long time since he felt wanted by a woman. He made a fist with his hurt hand and went to the kitchen corner and began to count.

"Ready or not! Here I come!"

Eli felt like such a fool, playing with an inanimate object. First, he checked behind the coach, knowing that Shavings wasn't back there. Then he searched the cupboards, and under the bathroom sink, yet Shaving was nowhere to be found. When he got to the box in the spare bedroom. He opened the box and found Shavings, right where he had put him.

He picked him up like a baby and stood him on top of the box. This time, Shavings was eye to eye with him. Eli looked at his features and admired all details that were carved into him. Except for the eyes. The eyes were dotted on with black paint.

It was Eli's turn to hide now. He cradled Shavings and brought him to the same corner that Eli counted in. There was only one place he could hide and not feel so silly doing it.

Shavings stood like a statue in the corner. "Count to twenty and I'll hurry up and hide." Eli reminded himself of the rules.

*****

The dark closet in Eli's bedroom was big enough for him to hide. He shut the door quietly and sat deep inside the closet. He was a minimalist, so there was enough room for him to sit comfortably. He brought his phone with him and was about to play a game on it, but he got a text.

"How did it go?" asked Ronald.

"How did what go? The Date with Omi?" replied Eli.

"Duh! You were supposed to text me how it went."

"It was interesting. That's for sure."

"Interesting? Explain now! Or I'll tell the manager that you played hookie that time Alexia broke it off with you."

"You won't do that."

"Did you get any or not?"

"I'm about to."

"What the heck does that mean?"

"She said I have to play a game before she will sleep with me."

Eli didn't read what his friend wrote, because he heard something. It wasn't dripping water from the sink. It wasn't the sound of his breathing. It was the sound creeping on his wooden floors. Something was walking near him.

For a second, Eli thought his hearing was going bad. He didn't want to believe what was happening. If he wasn't mistaken, the sound of wooden footsteps was walking around in the other room.

Eli's eyes were shifting back and forth in the darkness of the closet. Eli heard it again. Wood on wood. Walking around in the living room. Talking to Ronald about being intimate with Omi, was enough to make him forget that he was playing Hide and Seek with a wooden puppet.

Was this really happening? It can't be real. This is all a dream.

The thoughts raced through Eli's head like a bullet train. The evidence wasn't there to support that this was part of his imagination. It's true, the puppet named Shavings was walking around, searching for him.

When he couldn't take listening anymore, Eli was forced to go investigate the noise. He opened the closet door, then opened the door to his bedroom. The sound of footsteps stopped, and a shiver went up his spine.

Around the room he looked and found everything perfectly still. It was such a small apartment. It could only fit small sofa, a coffee table, a bookshelf, a tiny television, and a recliner.

Did he interrupt Shavings seeking him?

It was the front door that caught Eli's attention. The doorknob was tied with rope, to the floor with a metal ring. Eli turned the knob and pulled. It didn't budge an inch. It wouldn't move no matter how hard he pulled or pushed.

What is going on?

Eli was about to over think the situation but felt a piercing pain in his right shoulder. It burned like fire. He could see a small arrowhead sticking out of his front. There was Shavings on the table, drawing another arrow. The puppet hid and laid a trap.

He let loose another arrow but missed Eli by a hair. Eli was quick enough to dodge and weave, back into his bedroom.

*****

The arrow almost took out his ear. Eli slammed the door shut and inspected his shoulder further. His back was pressed hard on the door, so he could keep it shut tight, because there was no lock. The arrow was lodged in his shoulder. Eli couldn't lift his arm, but could still bend his elbow.

His cut on his finger was nothing compared to the pain he was feeling now. He knew he needed to call for help. His phone was left inside of the closet. Before Eli could shift his weight to attempt to move towards the closet, Shavings' blade cut through the wooden door and into his calf. The wood that made up the door, was paper thin. A beaded curtain would have done a better job against the razor-sharp weapon.

Tears and cries erupted out of Eli.

Shavings' blade ripped out of his leg and Eli fell to the floor head first. Blood sprayed out of Eli's calf and painted the walls red. Blood oozed out of the arrow wound.

Surprisingly, Eli was able to use his good leg to help move him towards the closet. The blade could be seen going in and out of the wooden door, creating an entrance for the possessed doll.

You're almost there! Don't panic! Get inside the closet and shut the door! It will buy you enough time to call for help! Pay no attention to the puppet that is trying to kill you!

Eli pulled the closet door shut hard. He wiped his brow with this good hand and picked up his phone. Blood began to pool below his leg. It's hard to think when your heart is beating so hard and you hear the wooden footsteps coming towards the closet door.

Eli opened his phone. He then dialed a 9' and the blade shot through the door. The blade almost went into his lower back. When Shavings went to pull the knife free from the wood, the blade got stuck.

The puppet kicked the closet door and kept kicking it. Eli then swung open the door and sandwiched Shavings between the wall and the closet door. Shavings body went limp.

*****

With one arm and one leg, Eli crawled to the bathroom and successfully made it inside. The bathroom had a lock and Eli made sure it was locked. It didn't make him feel safe, because he seen what the doll did to his apartment doors already. He knew the bathroom door wasn't any different.

He had to fight back. Otherwise he was going to die.

In the cupboard under the sink, he found some cleaning spray and a lighter in the top drawer. His apartment was on the third floor and there was a small window in the shower. When that puppet comes through the door, he will set it on fire and toss him out the window.

He began bandaging his legs as he heard footsteps outside. Shavings freed his blade from the door. Eli got on his stomach and lit the lighter.

This must work. Please! Please! Please work!

Shavings busted through the door and came through the opening.

Eli lit the lighter and squeezed the spray can as hard as he could Shavings got a face full of burning flames. The puppet silently shook in agony. His hat and cape caught on fire quickly and within seconds, the doll was burning and turning black. He smelled like burnt hair, which made Eli gag.

He finally stopped spraying. The flames danced all-round the bathroom. The toilet paper and trash can ignited. The bathroom was so small, fire erupted and jumped to Eli's hair.

The screams were loud enough to wake up the neighbors, outside of the apartment building.

Things weren't going according to plan, Eli thought to himself.

It hurts, but you can win! You can do it! If you don't do this, you're going to die! You're going to Die and Alexia will have been right about you! Prove to her that you're the prize! Survive!

Shavings arms were waving in the air and the flames were flying everywhere. Eli reached out and grabbed the puppet by leg and swung as hard as he could at the window. He plunged his head into the open toilet bowl, extinguishing his burning hair.

*****

Glass rained down into the shower and onto the ground below. Wood, fire, and glass made a satisfying sound when it hit the concrete and exploded in all directions.

Eli laid on his back and was going in and out of consciousness. His head hurt, his shoulder hurt, and his finger hurt. But his heart didn't hurt anymore. When was strong enough, he crawled back to his bedroom and back to the closet.

He picked up his phone and tried to open it. It was tough, because his hand was fried, and bloodied. It hurt to hold the phone. Eli couldn't help but cry again.

When he successfully opened the phone, there were missed calls and missed texts from Ronald. The first of the many messages said this:

"If you sleep with Omi, it might help get over Alexia."

*****

Omi woke from her sleep. She looked at her clock and saw that it was 3:16 AM. She thought it to be a blessing to wake up at this time. Many things happen during 3 AM. The portal to the other world is at its thinnest, perfect for the dark arts.

Before she could put on her slippers, there was another knock at the door. This time harder.

"I'm coming! I'm coming! Hold your horses."

The knocking subsided.

With a match, she lit a candle and was granted orange light, revealing her room.

There was a small table in the back corner, with a crystal ball on top of it. Next to it in the other corner, was a workbench and a pin log. A head was drawn on the side and front of it.

The flame danced as she walked down the hallway. Almost kissing the toes of all the marionettes that sat above her on shelves. It sounded like wood splitting as she walked at a quickened pace to answer the door.

She opened the door to a crack, big enough to let her face show. Her eyes were wide in surprise.

Eli was standing there with the box in his arms. His hands were bandaged to the fingertips. The bandages didn't stop there. It traveled up his arm and covered his neck and head. Only his eyes and mouth were showing. The right arm was in a sling.

Omi hadn't seen so much hatred in one's eyes.

The wounded Eli opened the box and poured the ash, wood splinters, and Shavings' head all over Omi's front porch.

"No thanks!" said Eli. He said it firm and convincingly.

Pain & Panic

By

Joey Beauchamp

&

Jorge Harrington

Afterword

Look at that, you made it all the way to the end. I sure hope you enjoyed yourself. We hope that you didn't get too scared. If you haven't figured it out already, Joey is "Panic" and I'm "Pain", based off the two demons from the movie Hercules.

Our boss introduced us, and the rest is history. Two authors with the same dream. That is, to create and share scary stories. This will be a first for both of us. Joey's first book and my first time being a coauthor. The experience has been a lot of fun and very stressful.

It takes a lot of work to – not come up with something original – but it's hard work to remember those hard times and put them on paper.

If it scares me to write it, then I must write it. That's the secret to one of life's mysteries. Look inward, instead of outward. It's that feeling you get when you hope you turned off the oven while you're stuck at work. Or the feeling you get when you drop your kids off at school and wonder if anybody is bullying them. What are you going to do about it?

We appreciate you the reader. We'll see you again soon.

Sincerely,
Jorge Harrington

www.ingramcontent.com/pod-product-compliance
Lightning Source LLC
Chambersburg PA
CBHW021933170626
46807CB00007B/3079